TEAM
ORGANIZATION

BY MATTEO PERNISA

Originally published in 2003 under the title *Organizzazione di Squadra* by:

www.allenatore.net
via E.Francalanci, 418
55050 Bozzano (LU)
Italia

**Library of Congress
Cataloging - in - Publication Data**

TEAM ORGANIZATION
Matteo Pernisa
ISBN No. 1-59164-086-5
Lib. of Congress Catalog No. 2004095754
© 2004

*Art Direction, Layout and
Proofing*
Bryan R. Beaver

Cover Photo
Richard Kentwell

Translated by
Sinclair de Courcy Williams

Printed by
DATA REPRODUCTIONS
Auburn, Michigan

Reedswain Publishing
612 Pughtown Road
Spring City, PA 19475
800.331.5191
www.reedswain.com
info@reedswain.com

CONTENTS

Dedicated to Fabrizio

It can happen that one day, whether you are young or old, you begin to see something from another point of view, a completely different prospective.

As far as I am concerned, that day was a rainy winter's afternoon in the year 1993/94.

The thing was the game of soccer.

The match was Reggiana - Foggia, the Mirabello Stadium in Reggio Emilia.

Nil-nil.

I was in the stands with my father, and for the first time I saw that perhaps behind what we were following on the field there was something, there was effort, there was coaching - there was a project.

There was team organization.

I understood that it was above all this that was actually being put on show on the field - beyond the anxiety about the result, the waterlogged field and the shaky classification tables. And, believe me, you could see it with your naked eye.

It was probably that very afternoon that I decided to become a coach - to try to become a coach.

It can happen.

Matteo Pernisa

INTRODUCTION

The first day of the get-together, the presentation of the team, the objectives are being outlined:

'... try and do as well as we can; save ourselves; a quiet championship ...', or for the luckier or the more pretentious '... move up a category, try and win the championship ...' and so on and so forth.

How do we arrive at all this? 'By our efforts, our exertions.' In three words: work, work and more work.

And here the COACH makes his entry.

How do we go about this work? Where do we start? How do we build a team? What can we give our team? What should we do and how should we do it?

Without claiming to find any state-of-the-art solutions, this book attempts to guide the reader through an analysis of all those factors that a coach has to focus on in order to define the tactical organization of his team.

How to build a soccer team from a tactical point of view: this is the ambitious plan of the book.

We start out with a basic concept, which underlines and gives form to the whole book:

Team play comes about through the interrelation between the characteristics of all its members and the coach's idea of play.

This is the mixture that sparks the team's play. The coach's task, both on and off the field, is to organize his team following a precise and specific plan.

There are four vital stages in this long voyage. First of all, the psychological department: why does a team require the presence of the coach? What are his tasks? How can he give his team the right mentality, and how can he persuade a number of different people to go along with a project that is his own?

The next step is evaluating the players' strengths and weaknesses: what should we be looking for in a player? How can we sum up each individual player in connection with his position on the field and the team section in which he plays? What are our operative means when we are taking stock of things in this way?

The next thing is to choose the playing system. Let us take a closer look: the definition and the requirements of a system of play, choosing the system and the consequent strategic interpretation in relation to the characteristics of your own team, picking out the situational tasks of the people that are to interpret it as you are working on the various movements of play, and, last but not least, the idea of tactical flexibility.

The last phase brings us from theory to practice. The exercises: how to set all this up. What means, what working methods to use? What type of programming and sequence should we use'?

If it is true - and we believe it is - that the role of the coach brings with it a condition of extreme solitude, and that whoever makes his way down this road sets off on a long and lonely journey, we hope at least that this book will make you feel a little less isolated.

CHAPTER 1

THE FIRST STEP: DEFINING A COMMON GOAL

'It is not so much what we actually do, but how and where we go about it that makes the difference. Perspective.'

... the first training session: not much talk, we do not really know each other, a set of individuals, glances, a whole lot of different ideas ... and a single guide ... somebody who is to show the way ... the coach.

Somebody who indicates the results to be obtained and how to obtain them.
These are the basic tasks of the person who is to guide the group.
The difficult thing is to understand where exactly we should start and what to do with each player in the group to make sure that they all reach a single result.

The result is the goal; you must indicate the goal, a final finishing line to everything that will be done and every decision that you make will go in that direction.

The club indicates the objective.
The coach's job is to trace out the way to reach it.
The players' job is to reach it or to make a good attempt at doing so.

THE CLUB   ⟹   INDICATES THE OBJECTIVES

THE COACH   ⟹   HOW TO REACH IT

THE PLAYERS   ⟹   RESPECT THE OBJECTIVES

The team's mentality is formed by the collaboration between these three units and the blending of these three ways of thinking and acting.

You build up the team's mentality by indicating one or more objectives, by putting forward a working plan and how to achieve it and by driving the whole group in one direction.

Having team mentality means interpreting all undertakings in a single-minded way. For this, there must be an objective to guide our behavior.

The final aim must come before everything and everybody - and then all our endeavors will respect our objectives.

Respect our objectives: reach our objectives.

When you have fixed the objective, your task as the coach is to study the strategy of all your moves, making sure that the great variety of points of view all point in one direction.
Personal needs and expectations link in with those of the team. That is why you need a guide who can indicate the direction to be taken, who can give orientation and establish rules. An institutional figure above the single parts who can manage the team group and who gives leadership to the players. There are two types of power and decision making in every group:

     · Institutional power
     · Charismatic power

INSTITUTIONAL POWER	RECOGNIZED BY THE GROUP ON ACCOUNT OF ITS INSTITUTIONAL ROLE
CHARISMATIC POWER	RECOGNIZED BY THE GROUP BECAUSE OF ITS ABILITY

By definition, the technical director of the team exercises the institutional power deriving from his position in the club, but it does not always follow that he has the charismatic force recognized by the group because of his moral qualities or his technical knowledge.

It very often happens that the charismatic leader of the team is not the coach but a particular player (usually the captain or an experienced member of the group with a strong personality).

Problems can come up when:

     · The charismatic and the institutional leader are not embodied in the single figure of the coach.

· The charismatic and the institutional leaders have different ideas or do not have the same goals.

As far as the locker room is concerned, the coach must aspire to becoming not only the institutional chief, but also the charismatic leader.
In order to do so the group must believe in the coach's ideas and in his working plan.
The coach must present the club's - and therefore his own - objectives, and he must lay down a working plan and a set of rules which respect the will to reach those pre-ordained objectives.

The coach must be able to 'ignite' his players. To make them part of things and to convince them that their project will succeed.
To do that it is important that:

· There is a project.
· The coach knows how to develop it.
· That he is the first to be convinced of its force.

How can you ignite your players?

The difficulty is that you are in charge of a great number of different people in the team, with different ways of looking at the targets and with different degrees of personal motivation.

The example of 'the glass bottle'.

If we all sit round a table, and the coach puts a glass bottle in the middle of it, everybody can see it, but they all see it from a different perspective, each one from his own point of view and the overall aim may not be understood in its totality.
This is the basic problem.
Each of us sees things in his own way.

Various observations lead from this:

The coach can spin the bottle so that the players can see it in all its various shades and tints, but as it whirls around it might topple over and fall, breaking into a thousand pieces.

Either that or the players could get up and walk round the table changing their point of view and widening out their perspective, putting themselves in another's shoes.
Empathy: putting yourself in another's shoes.
That will allow you to see things from different viewpoints, putting yourself in your team mates' shoes and getting nearer to why each of them behaves in such and such a way. Yet, in this case you might generate confusion because you would be reversing roles.
Everything would be more simple if the bottle was made of glass and if it was transparent. In that way all the players would be able to see the whole objective in all its parts even from their own point of view.
And they wouldn't start thinking that somewhere behind there was some hidden factor and who knows what secondary purposes.

It is important, therefore, that the objective is:

> · Clear and well-defined.
> · Transparent.
> · Totally visible to everyone.
> · Something that will benefit each and all.

This is the only way of getting over the difficulty represented by all these different perspectives and honing all personal motives into one single objective - because reaching your target will benefit all those involved.

Motivation creates behavior, and, once the coach has defined the objective, he must work on incentives trying at all times to communicate his ideas.

Each of us, and in this case the coach, communicates - whatever we do.
We communicate with words, but also with our silences; we communicate by being present but also when we are absent.
The very role covered by the coach means that he communicates his leadership, and every message that he sends out is an input that influences the behavior of the group, even when this is directed at a single individual.

10

So:

- · The coach is continually sending messages that will influence the conduct of the group.
- · In every message that he gives, even if it is private, the coach takes the whole group as his point of reference.

It is absolutely vital that the coach is able to communicate and relate himself to others.

The important thing is that the message arrives to the person in question as quickly and as clearly as possible without any loss of meaning. The message must be plain and there must be no shortfall about what is being said.

Remember that any excess in communication invalidates the message!

If you speak too much or if you are too repetitive, you lose conviction in what you want to say.

If you want to send a message to the team you must be:

- · Clear
- · Complete
- · Concise

CLEAR   ➡   SET OUT A SINGLE POINT IN A DIRECT WAY

COMPLETE   ➡   SAY EVERYTHING THAT IS NECESSARY

CONCISE   ➡   SAY IT IN A FEW WORDS

The team is molded long before it enters the playing field. A team that is well organized off the field will probably be well organized on the field. All the members of a team must be looking in the same direction and it is the coach's job to make sure they are.

It is very important when you are building up a team to be able to recognize the dynamics that regulate the group. The coach's job does not begin or end on the playing field or during training sessions.

The coach is the guide, and as such he must be an example and can only expect to get back what he has put in himself. It is not possible to expect others to be punctual if the coach himself is always arriving late. In the same way, you cannot ask others to be professional if you are not businesslike.

If everybody (the club, the coach and the players) is respecting the rules and trying as hard as they can to reach the objectives that have been set out -then you can say that you have created a winning mentality.

A winning mentality does not mean that you are actually winning. It means that you are all working in the same direction and trying as hard as you can. It means that you are taking responsibility according to your role in your attempt to reach the final objective.

OBSERVATIONS .

- Indicate the goals.
- Indicate how you intend to reach them.
- The greatest dedication in respecting the objectives
- Personal motivation secondary to team motivation.
- Ignite the group with your ideas.
- Show that you are the charismatic leader as well as the institutional one.
- Recognize the differences in personal objectives.
- Transparent objectives.
- Put yourself in others' shoes.
- Communicate in a clear, complete and concise way.
- Expect only what you give.

CHAPTER 2

EVALUATING THE CHARACTERISTICS OF THE INDIVIDUAL PLAYERS

We will now have a look at technical details - tactical ones being concerned with the steps to be taken by the coach in order to give strategic organization to his team. The coach's aim is to organize his team by blending his own ideas of play with the technical, tactical, physical and psychological characteristics of the players he has on hand. This is an extremely important balancing act in that, whether he tries to adapt his ideas about soccer to the player or the contrary, it is from this mixture that team organization begins and develops - and this is probably the most important factor in determining the fate of the season.

As a result, the analysis and evaluation of the individual players in your team is a necessary and compulsory stage whatever direction you are working in.

2.1 HOW A TEAM IS BORN

When he takes on (or presumes that he is doing so) the technical leadership of a team, one of the first questions that a coach asks himself is: 'What players do I have in my group?' His tactical construction of the team develops from the reply to this question. There are many starting points, depending on the situation or the context in which he is working (and this can vary according to the category), the level, the motivation and the objectives of the club itself. You may already know the players by name or from hearsay (though until you have the chance to coach a player directly and have him under your guidance for a whole year you can't really say that you know him) or you might be able to choose a number of players yourself.

Yet, these are isolated cases, and most coaches find themselves having to work with a group that has already been formed, made up of players that are more or less well-known, sometimes with the chance of slotting in a single 'piece' of their own choice. This will be their starting line, from which they will work out their own project of team assembly.

2.2 A FALSE PROBLEM

Should the players submit themselves to the coach's ideas of play, or should the idea of play be adapted to the players' characteristics?

To be or not to be.
In other words: who comes first, the system or the players?
A number of factors must be kept in mind.

- · If the coach is to give his players an idea of play, he must be the first to be convinced and feel that it is right.
- · If a coach arrives when the season has already begun and as a result has less time to work things out, it will be more difficult for him to change the tactical structure of the team.
- · If there is a player in the group who, when he is allowed to express himself in particular conditions, can give something extra to the team, you can work out a particular tactical solution which will allow him to do so.
- · If you give them the right teaching, a harmonized group will be able to play well in almost all playing systems.
- · In relation to the players you have on hand, you can change, not the playing system, but the strategy of play, or vice versa.
- · What really counts is the characteristics and the 'philosophy' of play that the coach is proposing - rather than the particular system he wants to use.

However you look at it, it is clear that you can do nothing without an initial analysis of the players' special characteristics. If the coach wishes to use a pre-established system, he must first decide if he has the right players in his group so that if possible he can find a remedy to whatever shortages there may be; if he wants to follow the second alternative he will once again have to evaluate the players in order to decide which system is best for them.
There are a number of things to be considered as we have seen, but only one way to go about it: evaluating the players you have on hand.

2.3 LISTING EACH PLAYER BY SECTION AND BY ROLE

Role: the attitude that an individual takes on in the group. This is connected with his particular function.
Every social system, and in this case every soccer team, bases

its existence (and survival) and its determination to reach an objective on the interaction between the individual protagonists - i.e., on the division of work - but also on reciprocal collaboration, resulting from the fact that each element shares a single goal. The players do not only have to play well, they have to play well together. Collaboration, a strong feeling of participation and belonging to a group, 'doing' and 'knowing what to do' for your team mates - all these are vital principles for team organization. Before you enter the field you have to know what part every single player will be playing and what role he will be interpreting. This is team play.

From a static point of view, you can define the tactical structure of a team in three lines of play:
the defense line, the mid field line and the attacking line.

Clearly, these three lines interact during the dynamics of a match, mixing themselves up and overlapping so as to follow the development of play. You can make out specific roles in each of these three lines or team sections. In the technical and tactical evolution of soccer, there have been changes not only in tactical structures and mechanisms, but also in the tasks and the compliance of the players, which means that the roles themselves have been modified. A number of roles have completely disappeared from the soccer landscape, while others have more simply changed their names.
The stopper has now become the center defender;
The third back is now the side defender;
We now have a center mid fielder.
We now talk about side attackers or mid fielders.

In listing the specific roles, we have kept in mind the most common systems of play and the real needs of coaches in today's soccer.

We will be looking at the following roles:

- · Keeper.
- · Center defender.
- · Side defender.

· Center midfielder.
· Side midfielder.
· Attacking midfielder.
· Forwards:
    - First striker
    - Second striker

In the complicated job of handing out specific tasks in connection with each particular system, there will be players with special duties or players with distinctive skills, such as a center defender who is better at marking (stopper) or at giving coverage (sweeper); a center mid fielder who blocks or one who sets up play. These are only some examples of special or diversified roles, but they are very important when you are building up the team.

2.4 EVALUATING THE CHARACTERISTICS OF EACH ROLE

What should you be looking for when you are considering a player on the basis of the role he plays?
How can you evaluate the characteristics, the strengths and limits of a player in order to insert him into the context of the team?

Generally speaking, you can evaluate a player by analyzing the four principle spheres:

· Technical characteristics.
· Tactical characteristics.
· Physical characteristics.
· Psychological characteristics.

The value of the player can be seen from the blend of these four areas, each one closely connected to the other.
We will now have a look at the technical, tactical and physical characteristics that the coach must be able to evaluate.

PRINCIPLES TO BE FOLLOWED IN EVALUATING TECHNICAL AND TACTICAL CHARACTERISTICS

In order to have homogenous points of reference for all roles, we will evaluate the phase in which the player is engaged (attacking or defense phase) and the situation of play with reference to the ball (on/with the ball or far away from the ball): see table 1.

ROLE	DEFENSE PHASE	ATTACKING PHASE
	Contrasting the player in possession	With the ball
	Not on the player in possession	Without the ball

TABLE 1

Evaluating the keeper is a little different and must be done using other specifics
See table 2

ROLE	BASIC TECHNIQUES	SPECIFIC TECHNIQUES	TACTICS
Keeper	Fundamentals	Saving techniques	Sense of Position
	Basic techniques	Coming out	Placement

TABLE 2

EVALUATING PHYSICAL AND PSYCHOLOGICAL CHARACTERISTICS

We will only be taking a brief look at the physical characteristics of the players, leaving it to the coaches and to science to evaluate these things on the field, and we will not be considering the operative tests that can be carried out. It is enough for the moment to study things with the 'naked eye': a brief, essential study in connection with the coach's technical and tactical needs. In the same way, we do not have the impudence or nerve to give tables for the psychological evaluation of the players. Even though we are firmly convinced that psychology plays an increasingly important role in a player's profile, we will be leaving this vital task to professionals, towards whom the skepticism that now reins (unfortunately) in the world of soccer should come to an immediate end - in fact space should be given for specific dealings of this type.

KEEPER

TECHNICAL CHARACTERISTICS

- Short passes with the inside of the foot (left or right): ball along the ground or bouncing;
- Long passes with the instep (right or left): ball along the ground or bouncing;
- Oriented control with ball along the ground or bouncing;
- Using his feet to put the ball back into play from the baseline with the ball on the ground;
- Kicking the ball back into play from the ball in his hand;
- Putting the ball back into play with his hands.

SPECIFIC TECHNICAL ABILITIES

POINTS OF REFERENCE FOR SAVING TECHNIQUES: see table 3

MOVING	HEIGHT	TYPE	SHOT TRAJECTORY
Central	High	Catching	Tight
To the right	Mid height	Pushing away	Spinning
To the left	Low		Bouncing

SHOT DISTANCE	LINE OF SIGHT	SHOT POSITION	PLAY SITUATION
From far out	Free	Straight line	Penalty
From in close	Covered	Diagonal	Free kick from the edge of the area
			Open play

TABLE 3

POINTS OF REFERENCE FOR COMING OUT: see table 4

HEIGHT	ZONE OF FIELD	POSITION OF CROSS	TYPE
High	Inside the area	Central	Catching
Mid height	Outside the area	From the side	Pushing away
Low		From the baseline	With the feet

PLAY SITUATION	TRAJECTORY OF CROSS	NUMBER OF OPPONENTS
Corner	Tight	Group of players
Open play	With spin	One opponent
1v1	Bouncing	None

TABLE 4

You can evaluate a keeper from the technical point of view by analyzing and blending all these points. Clearly, you will not be in a position to judge after one coaching session or one single match, but with the help of your technical staff and in this case with the specific help of the goalkeeper coach (who is now present in almost every level and in every club situation) you can try to understand what technical guarantee the keeper will be able to give you, after which you will know what to expect from him in relation to the play you will be using.
For example:

- Can I use the keeper for clearing with his feet?
- Can I create a quick attacking situation because his clearing kick is long and precise?
- Is the keeper having trouble with shots from far out?
- Does he have problems with high balls?
- Does he come out from the posts with authority on corners kicks or when there is a group of players?

By simply answering these banal questions, you can already see how the team's play can be influenced by the coach's conditioned choices.

TACTICAL CHARACTERISTICS

SENSE OF POSITION: reading play and placing yourself in such a way as to cover the goal:

- · To oppose a shot;
- · On a cross;
- · On dead balls (free kicks, corners, ...);
- · 1 to 1 situation, opponent coming right for him.

PLACEMENT: reading the action of play and covering a zone of the field in relation to its development. What you need:

- · Supporting teammates in the possession phase;
- · Repositioning himself in relation to the ongoing development of play;
- · Keeping the correct distance from the defense section;
- · Right timing when he comes out on an in depth ball behind the defenders.

The keeper's tactical characteristics are unquestionably those which most greatly influence the team's playing system. Today's keepers are players like all the other more mobile ten, and must collaborate and work in unison with them in each phase of play and wherever the ball may be.
It is therefore important for the coach to know just how much technical know-how and ability to read and understand play his keeper really has.
Does he speak? Does he help his teammates? Does he anticipate the development of play? Does he impress his personality on his teammates? Is he able to organize the defense phase?
.... ?
These are all specifics that the coach must look at closely.

PHYSICAL CHARACTERISTICS

- · HEIGHT.
- · SPEED OF REACTION.
- · EXPLOSIVENESS.
- · AGILITY/ DEXTERITY.

SIDE DEFENDER

TECHNICAL AND TACTICAL CHARACTERISTICS

1. DEFENSE PHASE ON THE PLAYER IN POSSESSION

- · Technical ability in contrasting with the ball on the ground and the opponent in front (frontal contrast).
- · Technical ability in contrasting with the ball on the ground and the opponent behind (contrast from behind).
- · Technical ability in contrasting with the ball on the ground and the opponent at the side (side contrast).
- · Timing his defense move.
- · Playing for time in his defense move.
- · Orienting the approach to the move.
- · Doubling up in defense.

2. DEFENSE PHASE NOT ON THE PLAYER IN POSSESSION

- · Taking up position with respect to the section team-mates:
    - covering diagonals
    - shifting and moving out in defense
- · Taking up position to mark an opponent.
- · Anticipating and intercepting.
- · Changing position in relation to the continuous evolution of play.

3. ATTACKING PHASE WITH THE BALL

- · Dealing with the ball in short clearances (right and left foot).
- · Accuracy in long or in depth passes (right and left foot).

· Oriented control while running or standing still.
· Dribbling in the 1 against 1.
· The cross.
· Shooting.
· Aerial play.

4. ATTACKING PHASE WITHOUT THE BALL

· Positioning in support or assistance of the player in possession.
· Tendency to put himself forward in going for depth or width.
· Overlapping.

PHYSICAL CHARACTERISTICS

· SPEED ENDURANCE (long distance).
· SPEED.
· STRENGTH.

Both the technical and the physical characteristics of the side defender will be markedly different depending on the tasks he is entrusted with (more a marking or more an attacking player?). The player could be more like a center defender or more like a side midfielder.

QUESTIONS YOU SHOULD ASK YOURSELF:

● Is he good from a technical point of view (right or left foot)?
● Are his passes and his crosses accurate?
● Does he put himself forward?
● Is he able to defend in the 1 against 1?
● When he is marking, does he keep the correct distance from the opponent?
● Does he show tactical intelligence in following the movements of the team?
● Does he react to developments in the situations of play?
● .... ???

CENTER DEFENDER

TECHNICAL AND TACTICAL CHARACTERISTICS

1. DEFENSE PHASE ON THE PLAYER IN POSSESSION

· Technical ability in contrasting with the ball on the ground and the opponent in front (frontal contrast).
· Technical ability in contrasting with the ball on the ground and the opponent behind (contrast from behind).
· Technical ability in contrasting with the ball on the ground and the opponent at the side (side contrast).
· Timing his defense move.
· Playing for time in his defense move.
· Technical ability in contrast on aerial balls:
    - The ball coming from the defense.
    - A cross from the side

2. DEFENSE PHASE NOT ON THE PLAYER IN POSSESSION

· Taking up position with respect to the section team-mates:
    - covering diagonals
    - shifting and moving out in defense
· Taking up position to mark an opponent.
· Anticipating and intercepting.
· Changing position in relation to the continuous evolution of play.

3. ATTACKING PHASE WITH THE BALL

· Dealing with the ball in short clearances (right and left foot)
· Accuracy in long or in depth passes (right and left foot).
· Oriented control while running or standing still.
· Dribbling in the 1 against 1.
· Aerial play

4. ATTACKING PHASE WITHOUT THE BALL

· Positioning in support or assistance of the player in possession.
· Moving up to give more depth to the defense line.

PHYSICAL CHARACTERISTICS

· SPEED.
· EXPLOSIVENESS.
· STRENGTH.

QUESTIONS YOU SHOULD ASK YOURSELF:

● Is he good at marking?
● Is he good in aerial play?
● Does he possess the necessary technical skills?
● Are his kicks accurate?
● Is he well-prepared from a tactical point of view?
● Is he able to lengthen and shorten the team?
● Is he quick to regain space?
● Does he have a sense of position?
● Is he able to guide the defense movements with authority?
● .... ???

The center defender is without doubt one of the most important roles - the backbone of the team. Besides his vital technical and tactical skills, the center defender must also have personality and charisma in order to guide his teammates from behind. Choosing and evaluating this player is particularly crucial.

SIDE MIDFIELDER

TECHNICAL AND TACTICAL CHARACTERISTICS

1. DEFENSE PHASE ON THE PLAYER IN POSSESSION

· Technical ability in contrasting with the ball on the ground:

- Front contrast.
- Side contrast.
· Playing for time in his defense move.
· Orienting himself in his approach to the intervention.

2. DEFENSE PHASE NOT ON THE PLAYER IN POSSESSION

· Taking up position with respect to the section team-mates:
- covering diagonals
- shifting and moving out in defense
· Changing position in relation to the continuous evolution of play.
· Intercepting.

3. ATTACKING PHASE WITH THE BALL

· Left and right foot.
· Running with the ball.
· 1 against 1.
· Dribbling in tight or loose situations.
· Crossing.
· Shooting on goal.
· Filtering balls.
· Oriented controls.
· Long and short passes.
· Aerial play.
· Ability to score.

4. ATTACKING PHASE WITHOUT THE BALL

· Getting free of marking:
- Dumping.
- Depth.
- Cuts.
· Getting ready to mark.
· Counter-movements.
· Assessing how to mark an opponent.

PHYSICAL CHARACTERISTICS

- · SPEED ENDURANCE.
- · SPEED.
- · DEXTERITY / AGILITY.

You must be clear about whether he is a strictly attacking player or one than runs along the flank because that will influence the playing attitude of the team.

CENTER MIDFIELDER

TECHNICAL AND TACTICAL CHARACTERISTICS

1. DEFENSE PHASE ON THE PLAYER IN POSSESSION

- · Technical ability in contrasting with the ball on the ground:
  - Front contrast.
  - Side contrast.
  - Contrast from behind.
- · Technical ability in aerial contrast on high kicks from the defense.
- · Ability to slow down play.

2. DEFENSE PHASE NOT ON THE PLAYER IN POSSESSION

· Taking up position with respect to the section teammates (diagonals).
· Intercepting.
· Changing position in relation to the continuous evolution of play.
· Pressing.

3. ATTACKING PHASE WITH THE BALL

· Defending the ball.
· Short passes (right or left foot).
· Long passes (right or left foot).
· In depth balls.
· Change of play.
· One or two touch play (speed of play).
· Running with the ball.
· Oriented controls.
· Aerial play.
· Shooting from outside the area.

4. ATTACKING PHASE WITHOUT THE BALL

· Getting free of marking in support of or assistance to the player in possession.
· Ability to insert himself.
· Reading play.
· Sense of position (balance).

PHYSICAL CHARACTERISTICS

· AEROBIC STAMINA.

There are different types of center midfielders: you can find mid-fielders good at setting up play, and those that block and destroy the opponents' actions. There are horizontal midfielders playing far back near their own defense, and vertical players who tend to insert themselves into the spaces.

ATTACKING MIDFIELDER

TECHNICAL AND TACTICAL CHARACTERISTICS

1. DEFENSE PHASE ON THE PLAYER IN POSSESSION

· Technical ability in contrasting with the ball on the ground and the opponent in front (front contrast).
· Playing for time in defense so as to orient the opponents' play (delaying action).

2. DEFENSE PHASE NOT ON THE PLAYER IN POSSESSION

· Taking up position with respect to the section team-mates.
· Intercepting.
· Changing position in relation to the continuous evolution of play.

3. ATTACKING PHASE WITH THE BALL

· Right and left foot.
· Short and long passes.
· Filtering balls / assists.
· One touch play (timing play).

· Crosses.
· Shooting on goal / dead balls.
· Ability to score.
· 1 against 1.
· Dribbling in tight or loose situations.
· Running with the ball.
· Defending the ball.
· Orienting control of balls.

4. ATTACKING PHASE WITHOUT THE BALL

· Getting free of marking in support or assistance.
· Ability to insert himself.
· Preparing to mark.
· Reading play / sense of position.

PHYSICAL CHARACTERISTICS

His physical characteristics are less important than his technical or tactical abilities.

QUESTIONS YOU SHOULD ASK YOURSELF:

● Is he constant in his play or are there long pauses?
● Does he give a hand in the non-possession phase?
● Does he play for the team or only for himself?
● Does he create situations of numerical superiority?
● Does he have good scoring averages?
● Does he have vision of play?
● .... ???

After having studied the characteristics of his attacking midfielder, the coach can create a particular system of play around him so as to bring out his gifts and make the most of his skills.

STRIKER

TECHNICAL AND TACTICAL CHARACTERISTICS

1. DEFENSE PHASE ON THE PLAYER IN POSSESSION

· Playing for time in defense so as to orient the opponents' play.

2. DEFENSE PHASE NOT ON THE PLAYER IN POSSESSION

· Position with respect to his section teammate(s).
· Changing position in relation to the continuous evolution of play.

3. ATTACKING PHASE WITH THE BALL

· Right and left foot.
· Shooting:
    - From outside the area.
    - Inside the area.
    - Acrobatic shots.
    - In flight.
    - After having controlled the ball
    - Dead balls.
· Oriented control.
· Defending the ball / Dump and rebounds.
· Dribbling in tight or loose situations.
· 1 against 1.
· Crosses.
· Aerial play:
    - On side crosses.
    - Flicking the ball as the defense try to clear.
· Running with the ball.
· Assists.
· Goal scoring averages.
· Long and short passes.

4. ATTACKING PHASE WITHOUT THE BALL

- · Getting free of marking:
    - - Dumping.
    - - Into depth.
    - - Cuts.
    - - Deviating runs.
    - - Feints (dummies)
- · Preparing to mark.
- · Counter movements.
- · Reading the opponents' marking.

PHYSICAL CHARACTERISTICS

FIRST STRIKER:
- · STRENGTH.
- · EXPLOSIVENESS.
- · SPEED.

SECOND STRIKER:
- · SPEED (ACCELERATION).
- · AGILITY / DEXTERITY

QUESTIONS YOU SHOULD ASK YOURSELF:

- ● DOES HE SCORE????
- ● Does he get the team to play?
- ● Does he put the opposing player in possession under any pressure at all?
- ● Is he good with his head?
- ● Is he physically strong?
- ● Does he give depth to play?
- ● Should you pass to him into space or to his body?
- ● Does he shoot on goal with both feet?
- ● .... ???

It is vital to evaluate the characteristics of your strikers when you are creating the team's tactical organization because it is these features that give rise to the strategy and the playing system to be put into effect.

2.5 OPERATIVE MEANS OF EVALUATION

Having now seen what to look for in a player, we will go on to a consideration of how exactly to make these evaluations. Here we get down to the real work on the field. Without going into specific explanations about the exercises, we will only be putting forward some ideas about working methods and making programs.

Apart from testing and coaching uncertain abilities, the preparatory training sessions should also be used by the coach to understand and assess the players' characteristics.

In the following, we will be looking at a number of working methods:

1. A match, 11 against 11.

If you have 22 players on hand, a full field match is a very good method: you set out two teams on the field using the system that the coach wishes or intends to put forward, or with the most common and easily understood system, which is the 4-4-2.
Without giving particular orders and entrusting the players with the roles that come most naturally to them, the coach will be able to get a general idea about the level of the team and to observe in as detached a way as possible the skills of his players.
He could also change various playing systems and even begin perhaps to change the players' positions.
It would be important for the coach and his technical staff to change vantage points: from above, from below, behind, on the field, right flank, left flank, attacking zone and defense zone - to give them different perspectives, the better to assess the players in their totality.

2. 1 against 1 playing system

In the center, on the flanks (right and left), near the goal, far away from the goal:

> · Frontal 1 against 1.
> · Side 1 against 1.

· 1 against 1 from behind.
· 1 against 1, with the defender trying to regain space.

Exercises in 1 against 1 playing situations are particularly stimulating and enjoyable for the players, and they are very useful for the coach, enabling him to assess the players' applied techniques (individual techniques) both in the attacking and in the defense phase.
If possible, it is a good idea to link up the 1 against 1 with shooting on the goal defended by a keeper.

3. Situations of play: 2 v 1, 2 v 2, 3 v 2, 2 v 3, ...

By increasing the number of players, you start to assess the principles of collective tactics in the two phases of play. Depending on the coach's aims you can make variations or set up particular conditions:

- Defenders in numerical superiority to help the defense phase.
- Numerical equality.
- Attacking players in numerical superiority to help the attacking phase.
- Limiting the number of touches to be used by the attacking players in order to encourage marking.
- The attacking players are forbidden to use dribbling so that they have to move without the ball.
- Restricted field size to put the defenders at an advantage and force the attacking players to use the whole width of the field.
- Greater field size to give the attacking players an advantage.

It is always better to use the goal and a keeper.
You can also add a second goal facing the first to give the defenders the chance to turn play upside down, which will give the coach the chance to observe the players behavior during the transition phase, i.e., to assess their ability to adapt themselves during the changeover from the phase of possession to the phase of non-possession and vice versa.

35

Whether it is a simple 1 against 1 or a complex 11 against 11, the match situation is probably the best means of assessing the characteristics of a player because it explores all the collective principles of applied techniques and tactics and supplies the coach with a great deal of information.

These are only a couple of simple hints to think about and modify according to your own needs, remembering that the coach's eye, his instincts and his feelings are vital to him and can greatly shorten the process of assessing a player.

It is to be noted that we have never used the word 'judge' because we believe that the coach is not a judge but an instructor/teacher. His job is to observe, to decide what may be missing, to understand the nature of the problem and then to intervene in order - and this is the most difficult thing - to find a solution.

A delicate problem is the assessment of players that have not yet been formed. There is the risk here of over-hasty evaluations that can penalize a player because they do not take account of the margins of improvement (which is something you should be looking for at every age) or of the young players' attitudes.

This is a book that sets out to give guidelines on the tactical construction of a team, and we strongly believe in good teaching based on the development and improvement of the individual players in order to ease the way towards the organization of the team as a whole.

The first thing that you must give the player is the know-how that he will put at the service of the group.

If a player is improving, if the players are improving, then you will see this in the team as a whole in terms of results.

To be honest, the task of motivating players is a difficult one: to go on pushing your limits, the desire to overcome them and improve. Creating external motivations and fine-tuning the motivations of the players are important steps in the building up of a team project.

CHAPTER 3

CHOOSING THE SYSTEM AND ORGANIZING THE TEAM

Having made his assessment of the characteristics of the individual players, the coach's next task is to transform all this individual material into a side. In other words: to give tactical organization to a soccer team. But what do we mean by tactical organization? Why do we do it? What advantages will it bring?

It sometimes happens that when talking about soccer we give a negative, scornful tone to the words 'organization' and 'tactics': 'The death of the imagination,' or 'The ruin of soccer'.

Once a coach said to his players:
'I think too highly of you and I respect you too much to send you on the field without knowing what to do and above all why you are doing it.'

In soccer, as in daily life, organization reduces complexity. We try to give tactical organization in order to simplify, in order to make play more straightforward, and this is the principle that we are to start from. Organize in order to simplify!!! A player must be protected and respected inside a playing system, and it is from there that he will emerge. The coach's task is to put him in the position where he will give his best, but that is possible only if you help him by simplifying play and making the best of what he has to do by coordinating his role with the rest of the team. The player must know what is happening on the field and he must have the expertise to be able to adapt himself to the changing situations of play. Skeptics must always remember that soccer is a collective sport, a team sport, and that a player's choice or the moves that he makes are influenced not only by the opponent but also by his own teammates. Individual play does not exist because you are never on your own on the field and each player is dependant on the others. It goes without saying, of course, that every player has to put himself on the line, give of himself. What makes the difference is the way he interprets play. But for the musician to express himself, the tune must already exist.

3.1 SYSTEM OF PLAY

The system of play is the basic set up of the players on the field, each assigned with pre-defined tasks.

It is to be underlined that players are never placed in a static way on the field; all we have is a dynamic arrangement that varies depending on the position of the ball on the field. When speaking about the basic line up and therefore the system of play used by a team we normally mean their placement when the ball is not in movement before it is kicked back into play from the baseline.
In this way we can give a superficial numerical aspect to a team (4-3-3, 4-2-3-1, 3-3-1-3, 3-4-3, 4-4-2, ...).

Requirements of a system of play

Every system, whatever it may be, needs to meet three basic requirements. It must be: RATIONAL, BALANCED and FLEXI-BLE.

Rational: it must be chosen and interpreted in relation to the characteristics of the players. You must respect the characteristics of the players who will be putting it to use.

Balanced: a well-adjusted occupation of all the zones on the field and a uniform participation of the players in both phases of play (possession and non-possession).

Flexible: it must be easy to modify or adapt the system without warping it out of all recognition to meet certain opponents or other needs.

Apart from these requirements, the system of play must be founded on the principles of collective tactics in the phase of possession and non-possession.

The Principles of Collective Tactics

PHASE OF POSSESSION	PHASE OF NON-POSSESSION
RANKING PLAYERS	RANKING PLAYERS
DEPTH	DELAYING ACTION
WIDTH	CONCENTRATION
MOBILITY	BALANCE
UNPREDICTABILITY	CONTROL

When you are talking about systems, and if you believe that teaching soccer as a game and therefore coaching players are elements based on understanding the principles of play - both in terms of individual and collective tactics - then you cannot afford to neglect the principles set out above. When a coach puts forward a system of play, what he will be coaching on the field are the principles of the game.

3.2 CHOOSING THE SYSTEM

At this point we have to choose the system of play.
On what basis do you make this choice?
What factors will you have to keep in mind?
What might condition your choice?

The coach will have to reflect on a number of things.

- The characteristics of his players.
- The aims of the club.
- The prospects of the club.
- The conditions of work.
- The system previously used by the group he is to coach.
- His own ideas about soccer.
- The time he has on hand.
- The application the group is willing to undergo.
- The field itself.

As you can see, the choice made by the coach is determined by a number of factors. You might find, for example, a group of people who, on account of their physical characteristics or their mental attitudes, find it easier to work in a certain way and to play a certain type of soccer. You might find young players who are 'lazy' from a soccer point of view, who will not be willing to accept new ideas or new coaching methods. The club's potential is another thing that might influence the choice of a playing system: what objectives do we have in mind? Do we just want to save ourselves? Will we be only trying not to give up goals?
Does the club's budget allow me to have players that will be suitable for a particular playing system? For example, if you want to play with three strikers, does the club have the financial

resources that will allow you to have such a large number of attacking players (usually the most expensive ones) in the group? It follows that the coach will have to choose the best solution for the team, based on the context and the needs of the environment in which he is at work.

Needless to say, every coach will bring with him his own personal experience and know-how, and above all his own ideas about the game of soccer.

The coach is able and is obliged to make choices, to decide what to do and how to do it, and his role is not simply to supervise the team.

Also, there are a many fine distinctions to be made, and there are many ways of being a coach and of visualizing that role.

There is no doubt, however, that the team starts off, grows and plays with the things the coach has been able to get across to it, with the things that the coach has managed to plant in the minds of each of its members.

The players' emotions are exactly those experienced by the coach.

The coach brings out a state of mind which inevitably communicates itself to the team on a psychological and therefore also on a technical and tactical level.

The idea of play cannot be set out or expressed only in a numerical formula, and therefore in the activation of this or that system, but it comes from much further back, from the emotions that the coach can get across to his men, from his own cultural awareness, which is then changed into notions strictly concerning soccer.

When a team goes out on the field, it brings the reflection of the coach out with it; it brings with it the image that the coach wants to communicate to the spectators.

The players will be influenced and guided by what their coach wishes to communicate to them. That is to say: it is not the choice of an actual system that makes a difference but its interpretation.

And it is here that the coach takes his most important step in organizing the team. It's here that you decide what path to follow in order to reach your objectives.

The interpretation of the system reveals itself as the strategy of play.

From a technical point of view, your choice of system or playing strategy is dependant first of all on the characteristics of the strikers in the group.

Theoretically speaking (and also in actual fact) they are the ones to score and so they will have to be put in the best position to do so, and the team's play must be adapted to their approach.

For example, if you have fast strikers there is no point playing with high balls or with crosses from the three quarters; if you have two tall players you will not be able to use a classic 4-3-3 with two wings.

Also, if the strikers are heavy weights, physically strong and good at aerial play, it is no use having them play 50 meters from the opponents' goal making them run into space, but you will have to use offensive pressing in order to regain possession as soon as possible so as to keep them near the opponents' area where they can make the best use of their skills.

These are only a few ideas to show how the strikers' characteristics influence the choice of system and playing strategy and why the coach must use tactical organization to put his team and therefore his strikers in the best conditions for scoring goals.

Remember that the purpose of the game of soccer is to score goals - which must also be the most important objective of the coach!

The coach's job is to find a way of doing that - by choosing the system, the strategy of play and the ideal methods of work.

3.3 STRATEGY OF PLAY

By strategy we mean the conduct of play used by the team to reach its preplanned goals.

For example, you might prefer an elaborate build up to a more straightforward vertical type of play, or you might think it is better to regain possession in depth rather than standing by and waiting
...
The playing system defines the static starting point in the team's line up; strategy defines the development of play in that system.

You can often find the same system interpreted in different ways, and it is in fact the interpretation of the system that sets up the team's play and the type of soccer that you want to put on show. Not every 4-4-2 is the same.

The fact is that not every 4-4-2 is molded by the coach in the same way because the trainer is different, as are the players, the conditions, and the objectives - the whole context in which you are working. The playing strategy is drawn up in connection to the characteristics of the team and its most important function is to make the best use of those who will actually be playing. The coach must discover what strategic approach will best be able to do just that.

The strategy can change depending on the opponents and also on the specific needs and problems that can come up on the field. Remember that you never play well or badly in abstract: you always play well or badly in relation to the context of play and also on the basis of what you have allowed the opponents to do. This consideration brings us to the idea of tactical flexibility.

3.4 TACTICAL FLEXIBILITY

Tactical flexibility allows you to modify your tactical set up or play-ing strategy for any particular needs that might arise.
You change in order to adapt yourself or to create problems for a specific opponent.
There are various things to reflect on first of all:

- · In the first case: why change?
- · Will the basic set up of play lose efficacy if we are always changing it?
- · Is it more difficult to merge the players together?
- · Do we really gain an element of surprise?
- · Will the players become confused, which in turn will create difficulties in the management of the locker room?
- · Why are there coaches who never change?
- · What advantages and disadvantages come from us camouflaging ourselves in this way?
- · Does an organized team change?

Let us try to put things in order.

The coach's idea - we could say his philosophy - of play comes to the fore when we are talking about tactical flexibility. Those who try to impose and set forth their own play against any opponent will be less inclined to change or adapt their strategy. Others are more elastic and less absolute and so are more likely to modify. One of the reasons for having tactical organization is to make the best possible use of the characteristics of your players, and flexibility can help you to bring out particular skills in relation to certain situations or to specific opponents. You change then to enable your team to express itself in a specific context.

What should be changed?

You can change playing system, but teams don't normally know more than one system well, and when I say 'know', I mean 'understand how to organize itself inside a system', because, as we have already seen, organization means simplification. It does not mean that you have a great number of options, but, rather, that you are able to recognize a situation, that it is clear to your mind what you must do. It goes without saying then, that a team playing with a large number of options and possibilities will never become organized and that makes it difficult to give tactical order to a group that frequently changes system. If you want to change you must try out the alternatives (and not too many of them) in training to be sure they are assimilated and can become automatic, all of which takes a long time. Even if you are simply going from a four- to a three-man defense, you will need a new approach and a very different method of coaching which cannot be explained in words alone or on the blackboard or in a single week. What we are trying to get at is that it is not easy to change even when you are in charge of players that have a good knowledge of all the principles of play because it is not easy to re-assemble a group. That is why an organized team will not normally change their playing system, or, at the very most, will be able to adapt to a few well-defined alternatives.
As we have already said, flexibility is one of the requirements of a playing system - by which we mean that you can make little changes and corrections to it so that its uniqueness does not get

lost. As he is preparing the team from a tactical point of view, the coach will have to study and train the players in these possible variants and the developments in play that they can create.

It is important to remember that you can modify playing strategy and still leave the system unchanged. The coach will choose the most appropriate strategy to use in relation to the opponents or other specific needs, coming up with the moves to make in order to put the opponents under pressure. The best thing is to give the team a stable playing base that the players can learn and make automatic, after which, as time passes, you can work out any possible variants.

In this way you are not running the risk of wasting time blending your players and getting cohesion from the team. The idea of tactical flexibility is a very up-to-the-minute thing, and many coaches look upon it as the new frontier of modern soccer, but unfortunately changing is very often associated with ad-libbing.

Being tactically flexible can have great advantages only when the team is in a position to grasp the changes and to get real benefits from them. That is possible only when they are underscored by specific preparation and well-directed aims. That, in its turn, will take time.

To sum up, we can say that:

- You can change, but you must not improvise.
- The more you change the more difficult it becomes to organize.
- The same system with modified strategy.
- Flexibility associated with unexpectedness (as far as the opponents are concerned - and not, as often happens, for your teammates).
- If the group is always changing it can lose points of reference.
- Flexibility is secondary even to the coach's concept of soccer (to what he wants to get across to his players).
- Those who are flexible can adapt themselves better to the different needs of the game or to the more general context in itself.

Looking at these points you will see that, as is often the case, there are advantages and disadvantages. The coach's job is to make his choices, or rather to make the right choice. Certain coaches are sometimes accused of tactical immobility, but it is important to remember that choices are not made off the cuff. You should decide on a project because you believe in it or because you think it will lead to results. You are flexible not only in the sense that you make changes but also because you are pragmatic, because you are able to read the signs and act in such a way as to obtain what you want even if you keep firmly to your ideas.

Very often the flexible person is one who changes without others noticing that he has done so. And that is probably the best way of all.

3.5 THE BASIC CHARACTERISTICS OF THE PLAYERS IN RELATION TO THE SYSTEM AND TO THEIR ROLES

We will now have a look at the most commonly used systems with their respective variants in relation to the characteristics of the players in the group or to the identity you want to give to the team. We will make a basic rundown of the needs and particularities in each system of play, and then have a look at the moves or classification that the coach will need to make.

The systems we will be examining are the following:

· 4-4-2 and variants 4-4-1-1 / 4-2-3-1
· 4-3-3 and variants 4-3-1-2 / 4-5-1
· 3-4-3 and variants 3-4-1-2 / 3-4-2-1 / 3-3-1-3 / 3-3-4
· 3-5-2 and variant 5-3-2

Unfortunately, for ease of comprehension, we have to talk about numbers.
The first thing to underline is the general characteristics of the players based on the roles they will be covering in the various systems.

BASIC CHARACTERISTICS OF THE PLAYERS IN THE 4-4-2

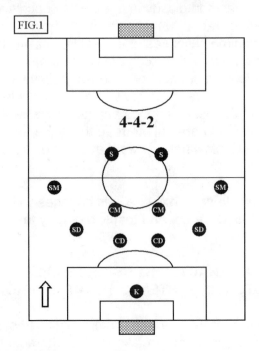

FIG.1

4-4-2

Center defender

- Good at front, side or from- behind marking even in the 1 against 1.
- Good in aerial play.
- Strong.
- Quick in regaining space.
- Able to give support to teammates in possession.
- Able to shorten up the team
- Good ability to communicate verbally.
- Good at following the development of play and moving with his teammates.

Side defender

- Good at front and side marking even in the 1 against 1.
- Distance player (stamina even where speed is concerned).
- Good at following his teammates' shifts and defense diagonals.

· Good at accompanying attacking play (able to break into space).
· Good at dumping.
· Ability in the cross.

Center midfielder

· Good at setting up play with short dumps or long passes.
· Vision of play.
· Sense of position.
· Ability to regain possession during a contrast or by intercepting.
· Good verbal communications.
· Aerobic stamina.

Side midfielder

· Good in the 1 against 1 in the attacking phase.
· Distance player (stamina where speed is concerned).
· Tendency to move back and form a defense block.

Striker

You can decide whether to play with two first strikers, with a first and a second striker or with two second strikers.

1st Striker

· Good at aerial play.
· Good at defending the ball and allowing the team to move up and into play.
· Good at shooting.
· Physically strong.

2nd Striker

· Mobile player.
· Brisk and fast.
· Good in the assist.
· Good at shooting.
· Good in the 1 against 1.

BASIC CHARACTERISTICS OF THE PLAYERS IN THE 4-4-1-1

The characteristics of the second striker differentiate this from the classical 4-4-2.

Second striker (also called half-striker)

- Good in the assist
- Good at breaking free of marking in the opponents' defense line.
- Good at creating vertical play.
- Good at creating numerical superiority in the 1 against 1

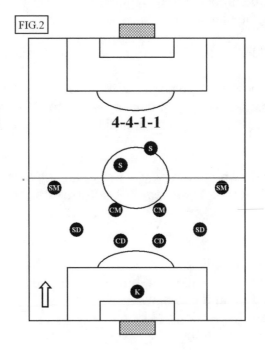

BASIC CHARACTERISTICS OF THE PLAYERS IN THE 4-2-3-1

The characteristics of the four defenders and the two center midfielders are more or less unchanged, with perhaps a stronger defense attitude on the part of the two side players in that section and the two center midfielders.

The two side midfielders have a more attacking role.

Attacking side midfielders (also called side half-strikers)

- · Brisk and fast.
- · Good in the 1 against 1.
- · Good in the assist (crossing).
- · Good at shooting.
- · Good at getting free of marking (cuts).

The center half-striker must have the same characteristics as the half-striker in the 4-4-1-1, and the center forward must be a classic 1st striker.

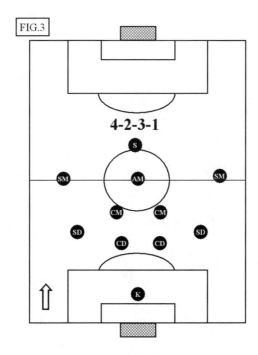

FIG.3

4-2-3-1

BASIC CHARACTERISTICS OF THE PLAYERS IN THE 4-3-3

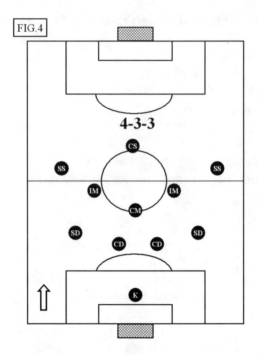

There is no change in the four defenders with respect to the 4-4-2.

The center midfielder or playmaker

- · Able to interrupt play.
- · Sense of position (horizontal player).
- · Vision of play.
- · Short dumps.
- · Long passes.

Inside midfielder (or half-wing)

- · Tendency to break into play (vertical player)
- · Ability to interrupt play.
- · Short dumps.
- · Goal sense.
- · Aerobic stamina

Side striker (or wing)

- Brisk and fast.
- Good at the 1 against 1.
- Good in the assist.
- Good at scoring.
- Good at getting free of marking (cuts).

Center striker or center forward

- Good at aerial play.
- Good at defending the ball to bring the team up and into play.
- Good at shooting.
- Physically strong (possibly with a certain mobility).

BASIC CHARACTERISTICS OF THE PLAYERS IN THE 4-3-1-2

The difference here is in the characteristics of the three strikers, or, rather, in the way they mix together. We will have:

A **three-quarter player or half striker** with the characteristics that we have already listed.

A **second striker** with the characteristics that we have already listed.

A **first striker** with the characteristics that we have already listed.

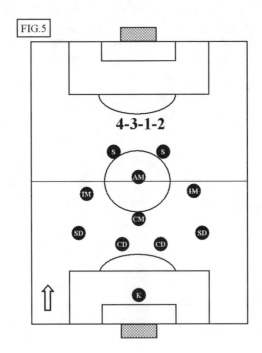

FIG.5

4-3-1-2

BASIC CHARACTERISTICS OF THE PLAYERS IN THE 4-5-1

The distinction between the 4-5-1 and the 4-3-3 is in the number of players that the coach wants behind the ball line, and so the difference is in the way the defense move into depth.
The players' characteristics are almost identical but it goes without saying that if you want the side players behind the ball line in the defense phase, then they will have to have different characteristics than pure wings.

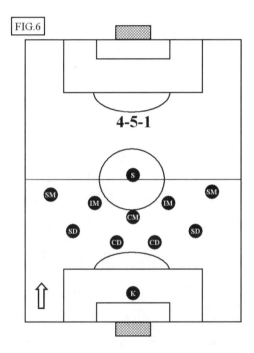

Attacking side player

- · Tendency to move back in coverage and form the defense block.
- · Good at the 1 against 1 both in the attacking and in the defense phase.
- · Distance player (stamina as concerns speed).

BASIC CHARACTERISTICS OF THE PLAYERS IN THE 3-4-3

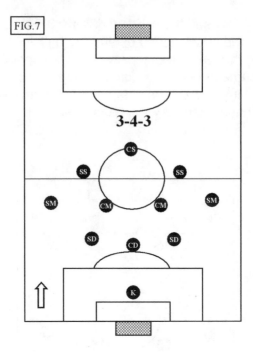

FIG.7

3-4-3

Center defender

- · Good at the defensive 1 against 1 - front and side.
- · Good verbal communications.
- · Tactical intelligence.
- · Good at aerial play.
- · Good at recovering space.
- · Able to make short dumps and long passes.

Side defender

- · Good in the defensive 1 against 1 - front, side and from behind.
- · Good at anticipating.
- · Good at aerial play.
- · Good at short and long dumps.
- · Physically strong.

Side midfielder

- Distance player (stamina as concerns speed).
- Tendency to accompany the team during the attacking phase.
- Ability in crossing.
- Good at following his teammates in their shifts and defense diagonals.
- Good in the 1 against 1 both in attacking and in defense (if that is possible!)

Center midfielder

- Good verbal communications.
- Able to interrupt play by contrasting and intercepting.
- Aerobic stamina.
- Good at setting up play with short dumps or long passes.
- Sense of position.

Strikers

Center striker

- Physically strong.
- Good at aerial play.
- Good at shooting.
- Good at defending the ball and keeping possession of it.

Side striker

- Brisk and fast.
- Good at assists.
- Good in the 1 against 1.
- Good at shooting.
- Good at breaking free of marking (cuts).

BASIC CHARACTERISTICS OF THE PLAYERS IN THE 3-4-1-2

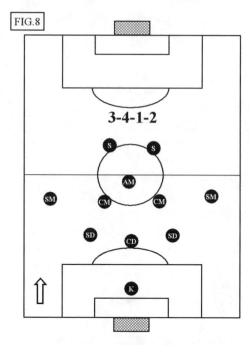

Nothing changes as far as defenders and midfielders are concerned. As regards attacking players, we have an attacking midfielder instead of one of the side strikers.

We will therefore be playing with a half striker working behind the two first strikers or the first and second strikers.

Attacking midfielder (also called a half-striker)

- · Good at assists.
- · Good at creating numerical superiority in 1 against 1 situations when space is tight.
- · Good at setting up vertical play.
- · Good at getting free of marking in between the opponents' playing lines.

BASIC CHARACTERISTICS OF THE PLAYERS IN THE 3-4-2-1

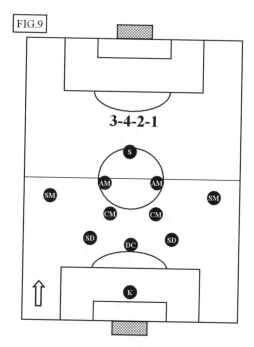

FIG.9

3-4-2-1

Here we are playing with two half-strikers or attacking midfielders behind a classic first striker. The players' characteristics do not change, even if, as there is only one pure striker, the midfielders have to be ready to attack space with more continuity.

BASIC CHARACTERISTICS OF THE PLAYERS IN THE 3-3-4 AND THE 3-3-1-3

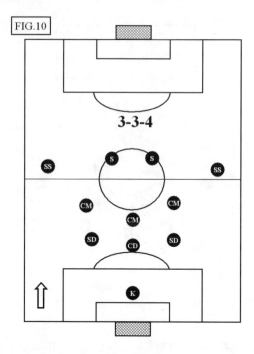

Attacking midfielder or playmaker

- Ability to interrupt play.
- Sense of position (horizontal player).
- Vision of play.
- Starting up play with short dumps or long passes.
- Aerobic stamina

Inside center midfielder

- Ability to interrupt play.
- Aerobic stamina (vertical player).
- Good at the 1 against 1 in the defense phase.
- Short dumps.

Strikers

There are two center forwards with the classic characteristics of the first striker, and two wings with the characteristics of side strikers.

A possible variant is the 3-3-1-3.

Instead of the double center forwards, you play with a half-striker supporting the top of the attack.

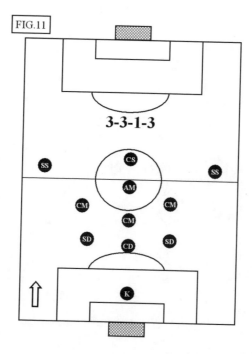

FIG.11

3-3-1-3

BASIC CHARACTERISTICS OF THE PLAYERS IN THE 3-5-2 / 5-3-2

It is easy to guess the players' characteristics.
The three center defenders will need all the requisites of players in a three-man defense (when you are playing either with a 3 or a 5-man line)
The side midfielders can have more or less aptitude for the attacking phase, depending on the needs or the characteristics of the system.

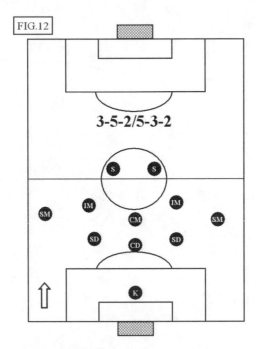

The three **center midfielders** will be:

> · A classic line up in front of the defense (horizontal players).
> · Two inside midfielders or half wings tending to break into space in depth (vertical players).

In front you have two players who will complement each other as far as possible.

Having made a global rundown of the various general characteristics to look for in the players of every system and every role, we
will now highlight the development and interpretation of the system in relation to the players' characteristics.

3.6 DEVELOPMENT AND INTERPRETATION OF THE SYSTEMS

· How to play to get the best of your team?
· What do you want to suggest as far as playing is
concerned?
· What indications should be given on the basis of the
system and the strategy to be used?

We will be examining ways of developing the various systems,
giving indications about possible interpretations (connected with
the characteristics of the players).
After that we will supply the tactical principles and / or the config-
uration of the most commonly used playing schemes in both the
attacking and the defense phase. Our intention is to define the
ideal tactical situation in which to put the player in possession in
the attacking phase, and, as far as the defense phase is concerned, the most useful way of building up common strategy.

We have said that playing strategy is influenced first of all by the
characteristics of the strikers, and so our rundown will start off by
marking out various possible playing models related to their particular characteristics.
At this point then, we will begin with the 4-4-2 system and its possible variants, exploring the attacking and then the defense
phase.

THE 4-4-2 SYSTEM and ITS VARIANTS

The 4-4-2 system played with two first horizontal strikers (double center forwards)

This is not a very commonly used system today, even though
coaches frequently adopt it during a match to redress the balance in a situation of disadvantage.

PRINCIPLE CHARACTERISTICS OF THE SYSTEM

Defense phase:

- On account of their characteristics, the two strikers cannot press in wide open spaces, but can only orient the pressing 'inviting' the ball out onto the side players.
- Because they are heavyweight strikers, they will not be able to play into spaces using speed; it is important, therefore, to keep the team's point of balance high so that they will be able to play near the opponents' goal.
- The strikers occupy the central part of the field, forcing the opponents to bring out their center defenders or to make long passes, so the side midfielders must react quickly in order to shorten up and they must be followed in this by their team-mates.
- As the team's point of balance will be high, the center defenders must be fast and good at recovering space.

Attacking phase:

- Use the sidelines to supply the strikers by crossing from the baseline.
- Side midfielders in depth to make the best use of the 1 against 1 and to stay close to the baseline.
- Side midfielders in depth to make the best use of the strikers' runs.
- Side defenders overlap to make the best use of the 2 against 1 on the flanks.
- If you cannot use width to assault the flanks and arrive at the baseline, you can also try long balls directly to the strikers.

Structuring the attacking schemes

There are two different strategic options:

- · The team tries to play with the ball on the ground, attempting to get into depth and cross.
- · The team decides to jump the midfield making use of the physical potential of the two 'pivots' in order for the mid-fielders to break into play.

With strikers like these, it is clear that in both cases we cannot use rapid counterattacks into the open spaces, but will have to set up an attacking style in which a number of players participate in the assault, going in to occupy the spaces that the two strikers cannot deal with.

As a result, we will have to play with the team 'short in front', i.e., with a number of men in the opponents' half.

If you decide to play from far back with the ball on the ground, you will need to do a lot of work developing overlapping play; you will need side defenders who are good at disengaging and putting themselves forward to overlap with the side midfielders in their own chain of play in order to create the 2 against 1. To do this you need to be short and in close proximity in order to change position, and at the same time the side midfielders must be well-prepared for the 1 against 1 so that they can create numerical superiority. Remember also that to be able to make the best use of your strikers the 1 against 1 will have to be carried out in the ultra-offensive zone near the baseline in order to cross and then use aerial play for a shot on goal.

A team that decides to play with the ball on the ground must base itself firmly on getting free of marking and moving without the ball.

The following are a number of situations that you will be trying to create.

Two players overlapping on the sidelines

7 receives the ball after breaking out of marking with a long / short countermovement, and, now free, makes for the area. 2 overlaps him without the ball, attacking the space liberated by the midfielder, and then receives 7's pass into space going for an assist, a cross or even a shot on goal.

It is important in side overlapping that the player in possession goes towards the area, while the player without the ball attacks from the outside (divergent movements).

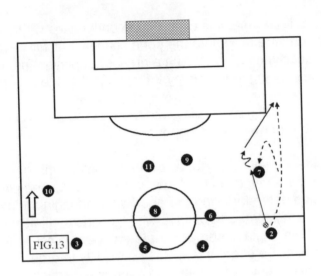

Overlapping with three players

2 passes to 7 and then overlaps; despite having made a counter-movement to get free of marking, 7 is being pressured, and so he dumps on the supporting player 6, who hooks the ball to 2 in depth ...

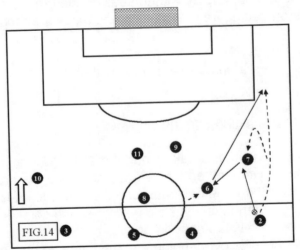

The compression of the players is important: they must be wide apart first, then tight and then wide apart again (the first two passes must be fast and therefore short, the third into the open space - pin ... pin ... pom!!!!)

The dump and rebound (or wall pass)

A midfielder plays to a striker, who, having made a long / short countermovement, dumps on a supporting player, who then hooks over to one of the two side midfielders for a cross, an assist or a shot on goal.

Having two static strikers, we cannot expect them to cut in, but we can play to bring the side players into depth.

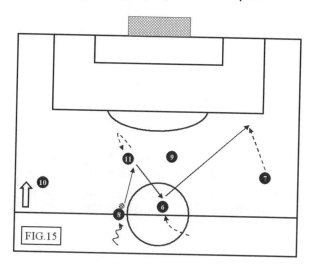

FIG.15

Change of chain

Ball to 5, who plays it out to the side players. 3 and 10 are under pressure and try to create space by changing position, 10 towards the center to meet the defense and 3 into depth and space.

The ball will be passed to the player free of marking. If we can choose, it is better to send the ball to the player running towards the goal and gaining field rather than the one with his back to the goal who is losing depth.

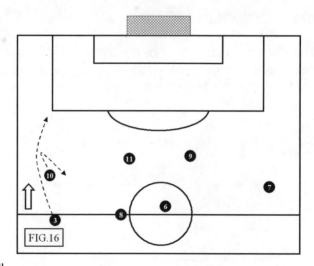

FIG.16

Long ball

The defender decides on the long pass to jump the midfield looking for the deviation of the striker who is coming to meet it towards the midfielder breaking into space hoping to get possession (and so in anticipation with respect to the movement of the ball - get in there first of all and then see if the ball comes to you).

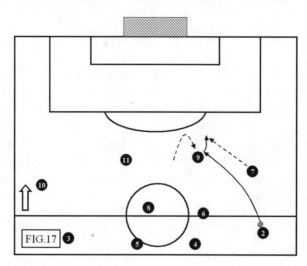

FIG.17

68

The 4-4-2 system played with a first and a second striker

This is naturally the best and the most common solution because it offers you more opportunities and more variation in attack.
As the strikers are complementary, the team has the potential for a wide range of options, and this gives it the advantage of not getting bogged down in a small number of attacking themes. If the attack is well-assorted and well-trained it can become very unpredictable in its play.

PRINCIPLE CHARACTERISTICS OF THE SYSTEM

Defense phase:

- As you are able to use space in depth, you can carry out pressing in the defense zone (it is a good idea, therefore, to keep the team short in the defense zone).
- You can even ask the more dynamic striker to disturb the center defender when he is clearing.
- Because you have two center strikers, the opponents will probably find it easier to move out along the flanks, and so your side midfielders will have to be good at disturbing the opponents' attacking play.

Attacking phase:

- There is a great variety of attacking themes, almost all usable.
- Apart from those that we have already set out, you can make the best use of the second striker's cuts into depth.
- You can alternate balls along the ground with high balls.

Structuring the attacking schemes

As the strikers have opposing and yet complementary character-istics, we can use all the possible developments of play, choosing the most useful and the most practical solution on the spur of the moment.
One of the most important developments will be the cuts made by the second striker going into depth.
Playing into space will be a particularly helpful theme added to those that we have already mentioned.

The following are a number of developments of play that can be carried out in this particular playing scheme.

Cuts

The side midfielder is free (or has broken free by dribbling) and he makes for the center, passing into depth to the second striker's cut into the blind zone (behind the defenders).

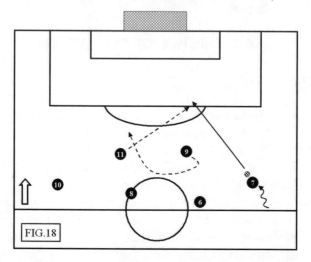

The second striker's cut can be carried out above or below the first striker, depending on where the movement starts and how closely the first is being marked.

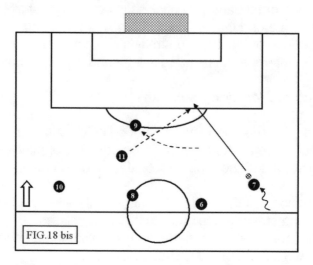

Dump and rebound on a cut

A midfielder or a defender looks for the first striker with a wall pass on a movement to meet him. The striker is being marked and dumps to a supporting player, who passes towards the second striker who has freed himself of marking by cutting into the blind zone.

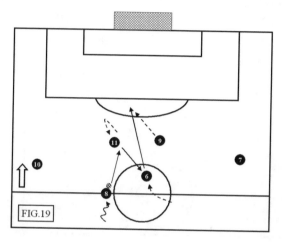

FIG.19

Getting depth

As the first striker moves towards the player in possession (he is the first to move because he is nearer the ball), the second striker makes an opposite movement going immediately for depth, possibly behind the defenders.

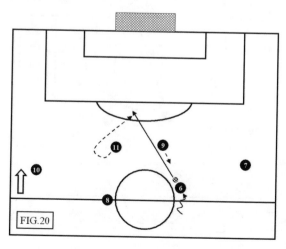

FIG.20

Deviations

The ball is sent towards the first striker, who flicks on with his head for the second striker's 'blind' movement from behind. In order for this to happen, the strikers need to be quite close together horizontally.

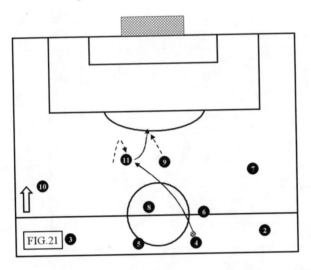

FIG.21

Feints

The pass goes to the nearest striker, who comes to meet the ball. He dummies the control and lets the ball go on to the other striker, who can shoot or pass back.

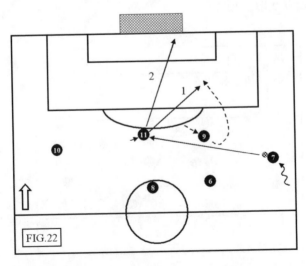

FIG.22

Dump and rebound on the side midfielder

The ball goes to the first striker (usually) with a long pass. He dumps on the second striker, who has come up in support between the lines of the opposing defense and midfield.
After that the second striker will try to put the ball into space for a side player attacking depth.

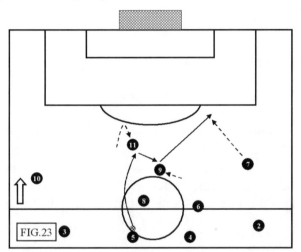

FIG.23

The 4-4-2 system played with two mobile strikers

When playing with two mobile strikers the best thing is to carry out breaks into space using the depth that the strikers can create. You should be playing if possible with the ball on the ground, and, once you have regained possession, you will try to send the ball straight up to the strikers.

PRICIPLE CHARACTERISTICS OF THE SYSTEM

Defense phase:

- You keep the team short in your defensive half so as to be able to use the breaks along the flanks.
- Low point of balance
- The attacking players must move back so that the team does not become too long, which would make it more difficult to move into depth.

Attacking phase:

- Play into the spaces using the strikers' speed and their move-ments.
- Go for immediate vertical play towards the attacking players who are trying to gain space.
- Use cuts and crossovers
- Keep the ball low.
- Think in terms of depth.

Structuring the attacking schemes

A basic concept in strategy here will be attacking space - ball into space.
You will try to leave a lot of space behind the strikers so that you can use depth in the blind zone.
The strikers' main movements will be long / short to surprise the opposing defenders by getting in behind them.
The following are some situations to put forward and use on the field.

Crossovers

The ball is in the possession of a midfielder or a defender who is running with it; the two strikers crossover, trying to break free of marking and gain ground in depth. The striker furthest from the ball crosses over by cutting in behind the striker nearest to it.

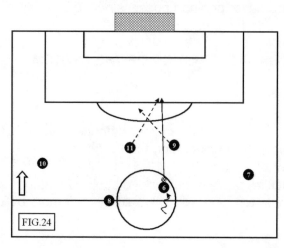

FIG.24

Deviating runs

When you are playing with your point of balance slightly low so as to have free space to attack, it follows that your side midfielders will be further back. In order to move up with your side players, the strikers will deviate out wide to become the points of reference for balls sent along the lines to be followed. In plays like this the midfielders give support by cutting under to run with the ball or filtering the ball on the second striker's cut.

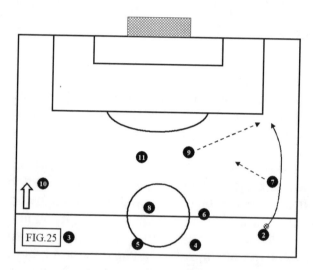

The defense phase with the 4-4-2 and variants (zonal play)

When considering the defense phase we have to ask ourselves two initial questions:

· In what part of the field do I want to gain possession?
· And consequently, how many players do I want behind the ball line?

We have already seen that the defense strategy depends on and is influenced by the attacking strategy.
It follows that where I am going to regain possession will depend on the characteristics of my strikers and on the number and the set up of the attacking players in the offensive zone.

If you want to press in depth, you must bring up the defense line and the side players will have to attack at once, which means that the whole team will slip forward, the strikers disturbing the opponents' attacking play and directing it out onto the flanks.

Be careful, however, because bringing the team up puts you nearer to the opponents' goal when you gain possession, but it leaves a lot of open field behind you giving depth to the opponent.

If you want to regain possession in the defense zone, the team will slip back to form the defense block covering all spaces and then going to hunt for the ball.

In this second case of stand by you do not concede depth and you cover all the spaces better, but there are two possible disadvantages: you allow the opponents to come too close to your goal (into the danger zone), and when you regain possession you are too far away from the opponents' goal.

A defensive 4-4-2 is probably the most balanced system of all because with 8 players you are covering every part of the field. The four-man defense line gives you the advantage of being able to defend the entire width of the field without having to use side midfielders in the difficult task of recovering space. The back section might have trouble, however, if you cannot win the 2 against 2 that you may sometimes have in the center. Nevertheless, it is becoming rarer and rarer these days to find teams that field two horizontal strikers in front.

To get over this dangerous numerical equality, the side defenders tighten in with defense diagonals.

We will now illustrate some approaches and some shifting defense movements that will come automatically and are easy to understand:

High ball on the side player

The striker positions himself vertically to the player in possession directing him onto a side player.

At this point pressing begins, called by the players further back (it is in fact the player more to the back that calls for pressing).

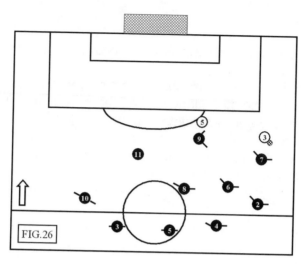

FIG.26

Ball on the lower side player

The side defender comes out on the player in possession and the side midfielder of the same chain comes back to double up. Doubling up is normally carried out by players of different team sections (defender / midfielder, midfielder / striker).

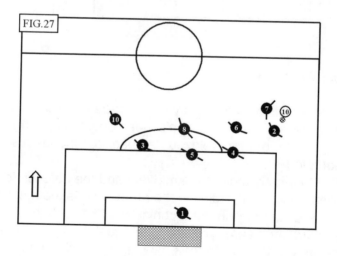

FIG.27

Central ball

The defense section will move in the following way on a central play:
a center defender puts pressure on the player in possession (marking him), the other center defender moves away in coverage and the side players tighten up diagonally to give coverage as well, forming a defense semi-circle.
So one is marking and three are covering depth.

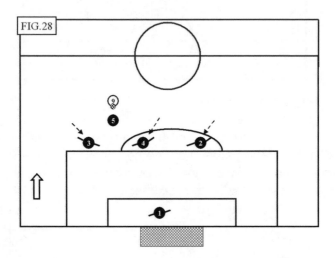

OBSERVATIONS

- Defense strategy is greatly influenced by attacking strategy.
- A lot depends on the coach's ideas about soccer (more aggressive or more relaxed defense, continuous pressing or not, etc.)
- The four-man lines of the midfield and the defense follow the same tactical principles in their movements though there are some differences in the techniques with which they are applied (the nearer you are to the goal the tighter you mark, the nearer you are to the goal the more difficult it is to switch, etc.).
- Offside is a consequence of pressing (if you press in depth it follows that you will have to go for and apply offside tactics).
- The two strikers have to participate in regaining possession, if only by directing the development of the opponents' play.

- With the 4-4-2 you have great balance, giving good coverage over the whole width of the field on all levels.
- Doubling up becomes automatic because every player has his symmetrically corresponding team mate.
- The two center midfielders defend mainly by intercepting filtered balls, and so they must be good at finding the right tactical position on the passing lines.

THE 4-3-3 SYSTEM

This is without doubt the playing system with the most varied attacking solutions.

PRINCIPLE CHARACTERISTICS OF THE SYSTEM

Defense phase:

- Having all of three attacking players, you start pressing in depth.
- The first players to come out on the player in possession are the three strikers.
- The team keeps short in front.
- The side defenders must be mobile because they have to be good at defending in wide open spaces.
- The inside midfielders must be ready to slip onto the flanks.

Attacking phase:

- The team is built up on chains of three players (third, inside, side).
- Using the whole width of the field with your wings.
- Principle of collaboration between players of the same chain.
- Developing play by using two / three player overlapping.
- Using cuts.
- Using change of play for the third striker.

Structuring the attacking schemes

<u>Three-man overlapping (one / three)</u>

The concept is the same as that seen in connection with the 4-4-2. This is a very good development of play for the 4-3-3 because it uses the natural ranking of the players in the chains of play. The play goes like this: 2 to 7 (A), 7 dumps on 8 (B), 8 passes into space for 2 (C). Variations:
> · 8 can play to 9 (into depth or with 9 moving back to meet him.)
> · 8 can play to 11 as he cuts in.

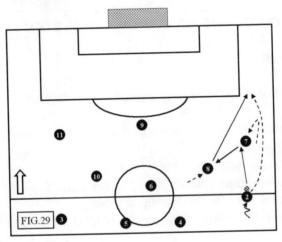

<u>Movements of the chain of play</u>

A fundamental principle of the 4-3-3's attacking phase is the inter-change of players from the same chain following these general ideas:

When the side defender has the ball:

The inside midfielder (8) and the side striker make opposite movements:

> · If 7's is short, 8's is long.
> · If 7's is long, 8's is short.
> · If 7 goes in, 8 goes out.
> · If 7 goes out, 8 goes in.

80

Examples.

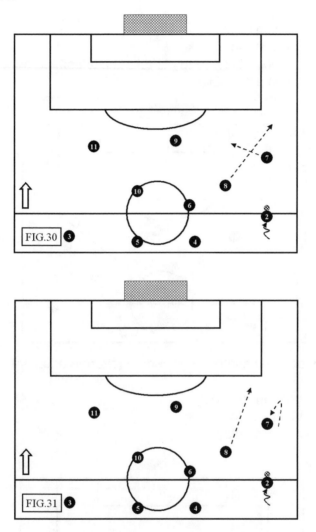

The most important play is for the side striker, who should try to get free of marking, if possible placing himself in a way that will allow him to head for the goal or get the team to move out (he must become a mobile point of reference).

With a change of play:

- · 7 goes in to attack
- · 8 goes out to attack
- · 2 supports play, ready to take a ball coming out or to overlap if possible.

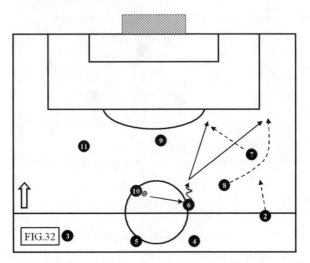

FIG.32

The parts can sometimes be reversed (change of chain):

- · 7 goes in to attack
- · 2 goes out to attack
- · 8 supports play

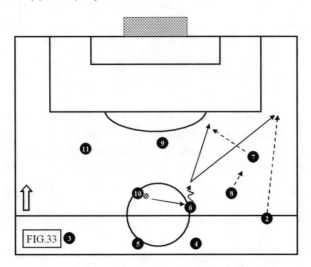

FIG.33

Or:

- · 8 goes in to attack
- · 7 goes out to attack
- · 2 supports play

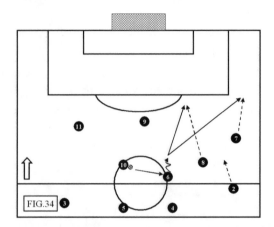

Once you have developed play, the following is another principle that regulates the attacking movements of the three players of the same chain: one above the ball and one below the ball.

Example:

7 receives but is being marked and cannot gain field so 8 sets off to make space above the ball, while 2 stays under it for the dump.

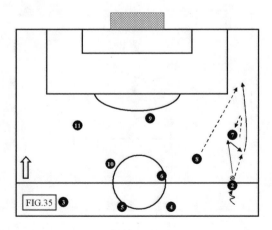

The center striker's movements

Because there are three points of reference in attack dividing up the width of the field, the center forward does not have to move across the whole attacking front. A lined up team has to get the side chain to move and to create play.

Example:

With the ball on the lower side player, 9 moves to widen out the chain's playing space. If the others have managed to come out with the ball, he will then cut in or away to support play and look for the ball.

Movement to widen out the field:

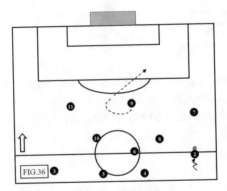

Movement to close in towards the goal:

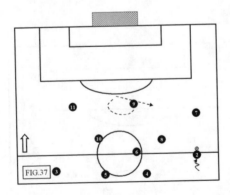

If the team cannot come out by using their chain movements, 9 will become the main offensive point of reference.

Cut over and cut under

9 cuts into space going towards the ball side; once the ball has gone by him along the flank, 7 turns and cuts in under the center forward towards the opponents' goal; having received 9's dump and rebound, he then brings the ball ahead to shoot or give the assist.

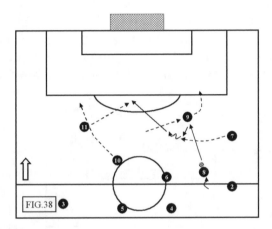

FIG.38

OBSERVATIONS

- It is important that the side players keep their backs to the sidelines
- When a player is standing still on the line, the ball should be played to his feet.
- If you keep the wings very wide, you gain range by giving them distance from the opposing defenders, allowing them to head for goal.
- With the wings a little tighter, you have a greater chance of cutting in to the blind zone
- The playmaker must always be in support of the action (behind the ball line) so that he can find outlets for play.
- The side defenders must take turns accompanying the attacking play (one detaches himself from the four-man line of backs) and collaborate with the players in his chain.

- The most important thing the strikers must try to do is the cut into the blind zone (if that is not possible, they come out to look for the ball).
- The deviation is not a particularly good move with the 4-3-3 because the three strikers are far apart and it is difficult to go and get a ball behind the defenders.
- Remember that because there are three strikers, you will need a lot of movement to create space.

2. Structuring defense schemes

We have already said that in a lined up team the strikers are the first defenders. It follows that the side midfielders will have to give coverage to the strikers and receive the nearby dumps. We will now have a look at some of the movements of the 4-3-3.

<u>Defense triangle created by the three strikers</u>

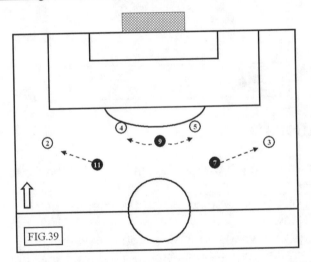

FIG.39

On a central ball it is important for the three strikers that:

- The center forward 'dances' in the central zone, closing off vertical play.
- The two side strikers form the lower angles of the defensive triangle, tightening the diagonal slightly towards the center of the field, and then moving out towards the opponents on the sides.

Shifting movements towards the center

The side striker is usually the first to go and look for the opponents' ball, and so, when the wing comes in towards the center, the inside striker must be ready to shift out to the flank.

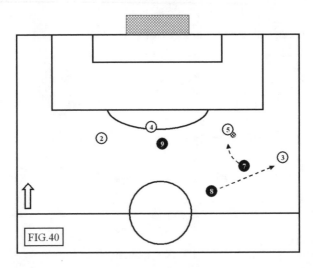

FIG.40

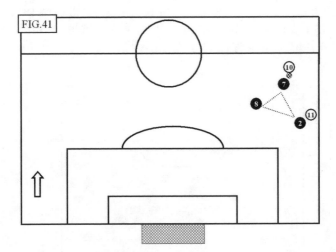

FIG.41

Naturally, when the action is near his own goal, the side defender will move out on the supporting player near the line so that the team stays tight; as the wing and the side defender get nearer to each other, the midfielder should give coverage towards the inside of the field (cf. Fig. 41).

Doubling up at the back

Looking at the last playing situation, it is easy to understand that 8 should help 2 so that 7 will be the point of reference above the ball when they have regained possession.

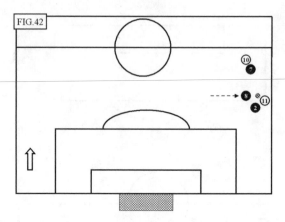

Doubling up in depth

When 8 puts pressure on the player in possession, 7 will come to help him while the attacking point of reference will now be 9 coming towards the strong side to disturb any possible central support on the part of the opposing team.

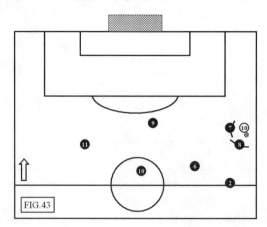

Defensive movement of the wing on the weak side

The wing on the weak side should move back slightly, covering the space open to the opponents' side player. He should not move too far back, but remain 'half-way', ready to move up if his team breaks into attack or ready to put pressure on his opponent.

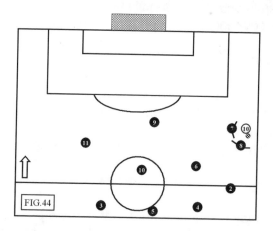

FIG.44

OBSERVATIONS

- The great advantage of the 4-3-3 is its natural ranking, allowing for the formation of defensive triangles without having to carry out any particular movements.
- The players are very well set out on the field, making it easy for them to cover all parts.
- You can play with four blocked defenders, but by doing so you will be losing many of the special characteristics of the system.

THE 4-5-1 SYSTEM

This can be considered a variant of the 4-3-3 even if it comes out of a completely different idea about how to play, and has attacking themes and defense movements that are poles apart.
Cover yourself, wait and then attack space!!!

PRINCIPLE CHARACTERISTICS OF THE SYSTEM

Defense phase:

- Defensive pressing.
- Low center of balance.
- A lot of players behind the ball line.
- Stand by, covering the field, and then press the ball.

Attacking phase:

- There is one point of reference in attack.
- You make use of the midfielders breaking into space around the single striker.
- Counterattacking play (wait and then break forward).

1. Structuring the attacking schemes

The attacking play is different from that of the 4-3-3 because you have only one point of reference in attack and, theoretically, you will be regaining possession further back in the field. There is only one striker, and he must be very mobile and able to hold on to the ball so as to allow his team to come out.
You will be playing a lot to the striker and then getting the midfielders to accompany the action, or having them break into space on the weak side.

Dump and rebound with players breaking into space

2 passes to the most frontal point of reference, 9; as 9 is alone, he will have to 'freeze' the ball and wait for support from one midfielder while another breaks into space on the weak side.
Because he is alone and normally quite far away from the goal, it is important that 9 defends the ball and waits for numerical superiority in attack.

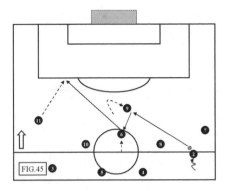

FIG.45

2. Structuring defense schemes

We have seen that as far as the 4-3-3 is concerned (and in a standard line up of the team), the three strikers will be the first players to come out in pressure on the opponents' ball. This happens because the side strikers and the inside midfielders play along different lines and the strikers are usually nearer to the opponents' defenders.

In the 4-5-1 the inside and the side midfielders are playing on the same lines and what happens here is that you come out depending on the distance from the opponent in possession (the striker nearest to the ball makes the move).

Normally the center striker will cope with the central area and the side strikers will see to the flanks.

Example of how an inside midfielder will come out

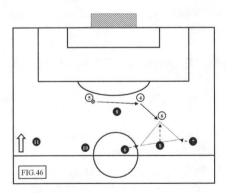

FIG.46

Example of how a side midfielder will come out

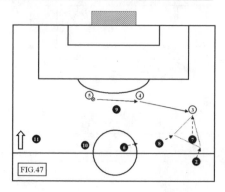

FIG.47

OBSERVATIONS

- The main difference between the 4-3-3 and the 4-5-1 is precisely in the way the side midfielders move out on the player in possession. It is this detail that influences the whole tactical set up and gives you the real vision of the placement of the players on the field
- You cannot expect the side midfielder to follow attacking play promptly and smoothly if you want him to double up with the side defender in his own chain of play during the defense phase.

THE 3-4-3 SYSTEM

On paper you might think that this is a very offensive system of play in that there are three players on the attacking front and only three in the defense line.

PRINCIPLE CHARACTERISTICS OF THE SYSTEM

Defense phase:

- As you are playing with three strikers, you will be carrying out offensive or ultra-offensive pressing.
- Short team in front (deep point of balance).
- Center midfielders always behind the ball line (giving coverage).

- Side midfielders must take turns carrying out the defense diagonal to form a four-man line (covering the width of the field).
- The three center defenders move only according to the progress of the ball and do not follow the opposing strikers' runs, which will tend to widen out the defensive net.

Attacking phase.

- You will not easily be able to make use of the whole width of the field, and so, once you have regained possession in the defense zone, you have to give immediate vertical passes to the three strikers.
- When you are in possession the three central defenders will widen out.
- During the possession phase get the side midfielders to attack without the ball (do not keep them crushed down towards the line of the three center defenders).
- As opposed to the 4-3-3, the three strikers do not occupy the whole width of the field, but keep tight and close together to make use of central play and the fact that the side players will be breaking in along the flanks (cf. the basic set up and the ranking of this particular playing system).
- Use three-player overlapping as an attacking theme.
- Use cuts above and below the strikers (when referring to cuts above or below, you take the ball as your point of reference - so, cuts above the player in possession and cuts below the ball).
- Use the 'pendulum' movement of the three strikers.

1. Structuring the attacking schemes

'Pendulum' movement

A high ball is played to the center striker, 9; the third striker (the one furthest from the ball) cuts above (going for depth beyond the opponents' defense line), while the second striker cuts below 9.
The most important play for 9 is to send the ball into the blind zone.

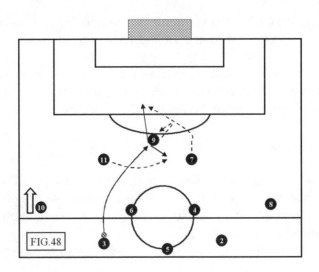

FIG.48

Three-player overlapping

2 is in possession; he gains field and, before he is closed off, plays the ball on 7's movement to meet it; as 7 is being marked, he dumps to the supporting player 4, who catches 8 as he moves into space.

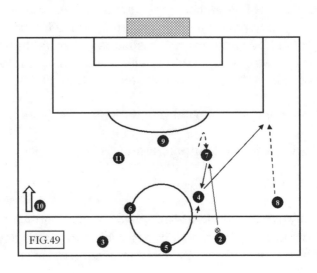

FIG.49

Cut above the third striker

11 receives the ball, and, having freed himself of marking by dribbling, he makes for the central area; on 9's arcing movement to
widen out, 7 cuts in to receive the ball in the blind zone.
(9 does not immediately cut in because, as you are playing with
three tight strikers, that would risk putting him out of the good
passing line as well as out of the visual field of the player in possession).

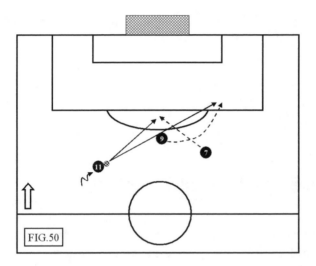

FIG.50

2. Structuring the defense schemes

With three strikers who can cover the whole width of the field,
you will carry out offensive pressing, keeping the team short in
front. As a result, you will be conceding depth behind the defense
line. The difference between a real three-man defense and a five
man defense is in the moves to give coverage on the part of the
side midfielders. The principles of the three-man defense foresee
that only one side midfielder (the one placed on the weak flank)
should carry out the diagonal to make up a four-man line. It follows that the central backs of the three-man defense do not only
defend in the central zone, but shift along to attack the opponent,
even on the sidelines.

An example of a defense shift (Fig. 51)

As you can see in the figure, it is the left center defender who moves up to the midfield and not the inside midfielder who moves back, which would greatly lower the team's center of balance.

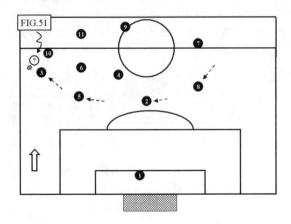

Shifting movement of the inside midfielder

In this case it is the center midfielder who shifts out onto the side. If you select this second option as the main defense movement, you are choosing to bring the team much lower and give greater coverage in the central zone.

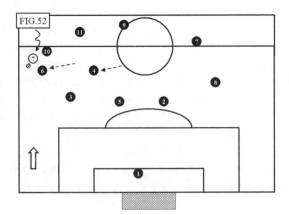

The side midfielder's diagonal movement on the weak flank

Depending on the coach's instructions, 8's diagonal move can be in line with the center midfielder, more forward, or even covering him (though that might be laying it on a bit thick and would be difficult to carry out). On 8's diagonal movement to tighten in, the striker in the same chain of play should move slightly backwards to line up the distance and become a point of reference in attack should the team regain possession.

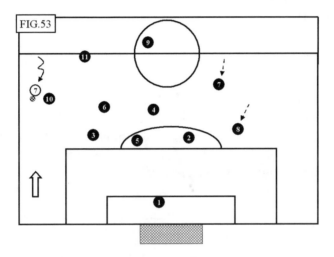

We will now try to reply to the question: how can the three central defenders move?

● ZONALLY

You come out to mark in your own zone of competence; so, on the center right the right back comes out and the center defender gives coverage. The same principle is applied symmetrically on the left.
The center defender will come out to mark in the center with the two other defenders at the side, forming the defensive triangle to give coverage. (Fig. 54)

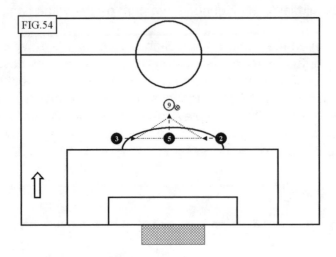

● MAN TO MAN MARKING

The side defenders will have the job of marking their pre-established opposing strikers, exchanging zones of competence (the center defender acts as a sweeper).

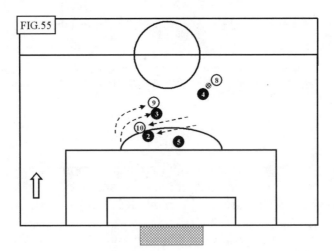

● MAN TO MAN MARKING IN THE ZONE

The side defenders mark in their own zones of competence (right or left), and the center defender will always be giving coverage to his team mate in action.

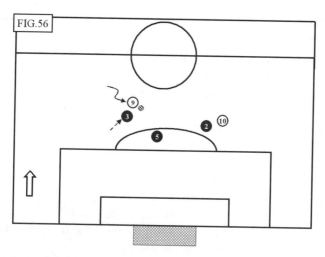

FIG.56

THE 3-4-1-2 SYSTEM

This is a variation of the 3-4-3 with the presence of a player, commonly called the playmaker or fantasy player, free to move between the midfield and the opponents' defense line. If you want this type of player to express himself, give his best and (most important of all) improve the performance of his team, it is a good idea to place him in the team set up with just a few well-defined tasks in the defense phase.

PRINCIPLE CHARACTERISTICS OF THE SYSTEM

Defense phase:

- ● You can decide where to carry out defensive pressing in relation to the tasks assigned to the fantasy player.
- ● The concepts and the principles applied to defense shifts are similar to those of the 3-4-3.
- ● Center midfielders are always behind the ball line.

Attacking phase:

- Use dump and rebound passes and try to play into space.
- Use cuts.
- The fantasy player must try to break into the spaces left free by the strikers.
- The side midfielders must try to break into space.
- Use crossovers
- It is important that the fantasy player should be able to get free of marking; he must go and look for the right spaces in order to do so and to be able to create play.

Structuring attacking schemes

<u>Dump and rebound followed by an attempt to create space</u>

Dump on 9, rebounding on 10, who has freed himself of marking in between the lines; he filters the ball into the blind zone for the second striker's cut (most important type of play); or sends the ball into space to catch a side midfielder.

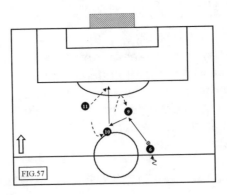

FIG.57

<u>The fantasy player breaks in</u>

A midfielder moves up and plays to the first striker coming back to meet him; he is being marked and dumps to a center midfielder.
These plays are for the opposing in-depth movements of the second striker and the fantasy player. (Fig. 58)

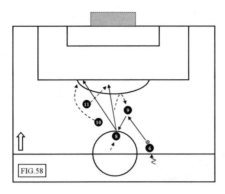

FIG.58

Running with the ball and then filtering it through with a movement to widen out

Having been served by a midfielder, 10 can move forward; the two strikers are close together and so they widen out moving across the field and then into depth to create space for 10 to run with the ball. The fantasy player can then decide whether to continue the play himself, or go for an in-depth assist to the strikers.

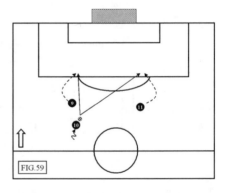

FIG.59

Running with the ball and then filtering it through with the strikers' crossover movement

10 is free to make for the opponents' goal and he can choose the play to make on one of the two strikers who are crossing over.

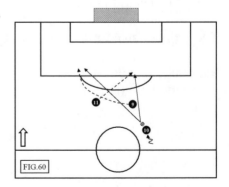

FIG.60

2. Structuring the defensive schemes

The point is this: what do we do with the two strikers and the fantasy player during the defense phase?
In other words: what should we ask the fantasy player to do during the defense phase?

Options:
> A. Widen out the two strikers and let the fantasy player come out centrally on their line.

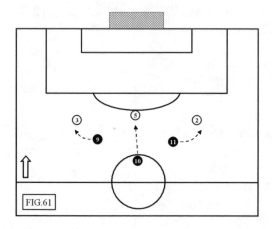

FIG.61

At this point you have a three-man attack and so a defense situation that is similar to the 3-4-3.

> B. Bring the attacking player out on the weak side.

The strikers shift towards the area where the opponents orient the beginning of their play, and the fantasy player shifts towards the opposite side, ready to come out if the ball is passed back along the line. (Fig. 62)

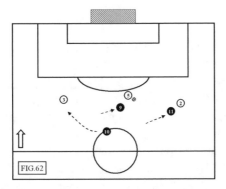

FIG.62

C. Bring the fantasy player back onto the line of midfielders towards the center or out on the flanks.

Here you get a midfield line of five players.
The fantasy player can move back to the center between the two
center midfielders or towards the flanks on the weak side.

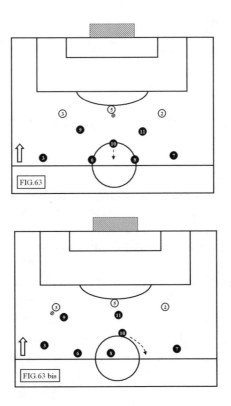

FIG.63

FIG.63 bis

OBSERVATIONS

- Having a player who is very free tactically speaking can create unpredictability for the opponents, but also for his own team if he is not organized well and given good support.
- A three-man defense is not more penetrable than a four-man one if the side midfielders work to integrate themselves in it - quite the opposite!
- The fantasy player must not play off-center or too far back - he would become a non-factor in attack.
- If your center striker is very big and not very mobile, it would perhaps be better during the defense phase to bring the fantasy player out on the line of strikers away from the center (either on the strong or the weak side).
- If you decide to bring the fantasy player back to the midfield, you will greatly lower your team's center of balance and concede a lot of space to the opponents.

THE 4-2-3-1 SYSTEM

This is also called the 'French' system.
The advantage is that a lot of attacking players can co-exist without losing balance.

PRINCIPLE CHARACTERISTICS OF THE SYSTEM

Defense phase:

- 6 players (4 defenders and 2 center midfielders) whose specific job it is to look after the defense phase.
- Team will inevitably break in two.
- Use the three half-strikers as a bridge and to help cover free space.
- The side defenders are blocked.
- The side defenders will have to be good in the non-possession phase because they will not be supported or assisted by the side attacking players doubling up.

Attacking phase:

- 4 players whose specific job it is to look after the attacking phase.
- Use cuts.
- You look for and gain numerical superiority in the half-strikers' 1 against 1.
- Side defenders do not overlap (the team is broken in two).
- The center half-striker looks for space in front of and behind the center forward.
- The center midfielders must always give support to the attacking plays.

1. Structuring the attacking schemes

One touch play by the attacking midfielder

Having made a countermovement, 10 comes to meet 2 and get the ball from him; he immediately plays it along the line for the side striker 7. It is important that when 10 goes to take the ball he is 'open' in relation to 7.

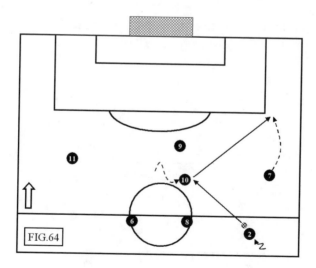

FIG.64

The half-striker giving support to the center forward

After receiving the ball, because he is being marked, 9 dumps to 10, who catches a side player in the space.
As play progresses, 9 is always the most forward attacking point of reference.

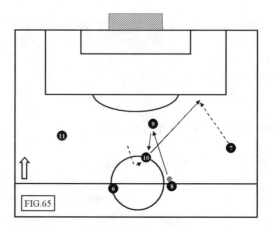

FIG.65

The half-striker's movement into depth above the center forward

9 dumps to a supporting player who plays on to 10, who has broken free of marking by moving into depth behind the center forward.

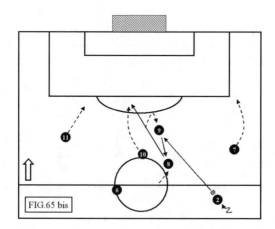

FIG.65 bis

2. Structuring the defense schemes

We have already said that this playing system will inevitably break the team in two, putting the defense phase into the hands of 6 players and leave the attacking phase to the remaining 4. Nevertheless, there must be some collaboration if you want to create the necessary balance. In this direction the work of the three half-strikers will be particularly important. They will have to carry out the movements that will connect the two parts of the team, not only in the defense phase but also at the moment when possession is regained and in the build up.

Even though you cannot ask the side strikers to double up systematically to assist the side defenders, it is still very important for them to move back and get nearer to their back line to tighten up distances and to act as attacking points of reference when the team makes a break.

Coming out of the line of attack

10 acts as a second striker coming up to put pressure on the opposing center defenders, creating a sort of 4-4-2.

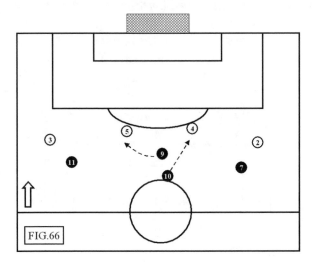

FIG.66

Coming back to the midfield

10 moves back centrally to the line of midfielders, between the two center midfielders, creating a sort of 4-3-3.

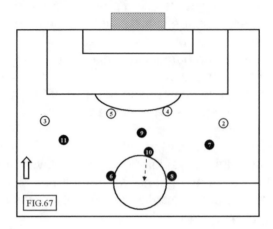

FIG.67

OBSERVATIONS

- What principally distinguishes this playing system from the more classic 4-4-2 or the 4-4-1-1 are the attacking movements of the in depth side players (7 and 11). When the 4-4-2 and the 4-4-1-1 are lined up, the side players do not cut in because the space in the center is occupied by the two strikers. Instead, this is a very common movement of the 4-2-3-1, similar to that made by the wings in the 4-3-3.

Cut to enter in the 4-2-3-1

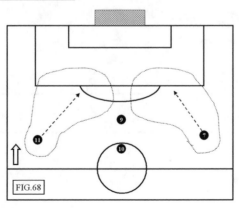

FIG.68

The following is a presentation of the various movements made by the side attacking players:

Cutting in

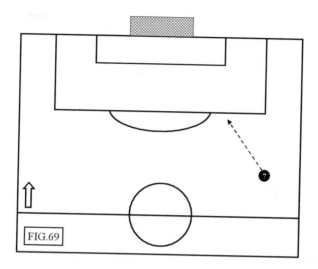

FIG.69

Cutting to receive

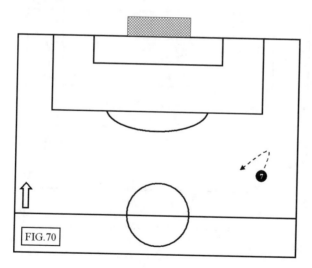

FIG.70

Movement into depth

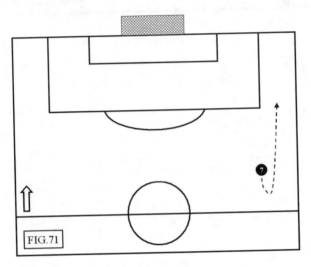

FIG.71

Movement to meet

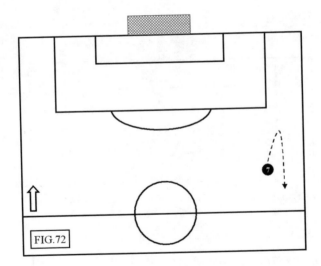

FIG.72

THE 4-3-1-2 SYSTEM

This can be considered a variant of the 4-3-3 or a 4-4-2 played in rhombus formation.

PRINCIPLE CHARACTERISTICS OF THE SYSTEM

Defense phase:

- The team's center of balance will be higher or lower depending on the position of the three-quarter player.
- The team will tend to lengthen out if the three-quarter player does not connect the line of attack with that of the midfield.
- The defense and the midfield lines must play very close together to cover the width of the field.
- The side players of the defense must be ready to join the three-player midfield line.

Attacking phase:

- You play low balls to get the three-quarter player into play.
- The three-quarter player must not get crushed into the line of strikers.
- Two mobile strikers good at dump and rebounds and cuts.
- Inside midfielders and side defenders give width to play depending on whether you have four blocked defenders, or the side backs taking turns going into play.
- Breaks are very important, with the three-quarter player able to aim for the opponents' defense.
- The strikers look for depth to lengthen out the opponents and allow the three-quarter player to find space between the lines.

1. Structuring the attacking schemes

The strikers move to gain width

10 is running with the ball in the center, and the two strikers get free of marking by widening out to expand the opponents' defense and loosen their marking.
10 can go for the 1 against 1 in the center of the defense to shoot or to put the ball in on one of the strikers' cuts. (Fig. 73)

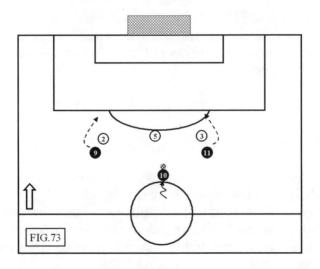

FIG.73

Change of play for the inside midfielder

With the ball making the rounds of the midfield from the right, the three-quarter player moves back; the second striker cuts in and the left inside midfielder opens out to receive the change of play from the center midfielder. He can go for the cross, run with the ball himself or penetrate with a one-two.

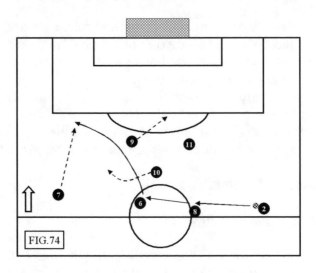

FIG.74

All the attacking themes that we have already presented for the 3-4-1-2 are valid here as well, and in all systems that have two strikers and a three-quarter player:

- Dump and rebound for the three-quarter player, who catches the second striker as he cuts;
- The first striker deviates for the second striker or the three-quarter player, who is breaking into space in the hope of getting the ball.

Note that during the attacking phase you have to lengthen out the team a great deal, playing in a rhombus formation, in order to make the best possible use of the three hypothetical lines that are created in the midfield. In this way it becomes difficult for the opponents to block the two most important sources of play: the leading center defender and / or the three-quarter player. It is vital, therefore, that these two do not get crushed into a single line, but that they play on different rows, and that will only be possible if the team is good at opening up and lengthening out when they are in possession to create playing space.

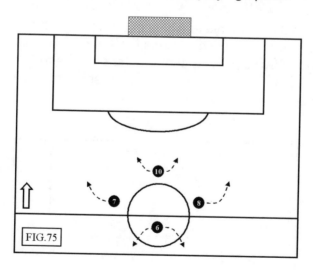

FIG.75

2. Structuring the defense schemes

Here again the organization of play is similar to other systems that have two strikers with a three-quarter player behind them. Two important aspects should be underlined:

1. The team will be able to take up an attitude that is more or less aggressive in regaining possession depending on whether the three-quarter player positions himself on the attacking line or on the midfield line during the phase of non-possession.
2. Whether he gets in line with the strikers or the midfielders, the three-quarter player will always be able to move back into the central zone or onto the flanks (usually on the weak side).

An analysis of the possibilities open to the three-quarter player:

A. The three-quarter player lines up centrally with the strikers.

In this case, the two strikers widen out covering the field in width, and the three-quarter player inserts himself on the strikers' line disturbing the two opposing center defenders. As they now have three players in front, the team will try to regain possession in the attacking zone.

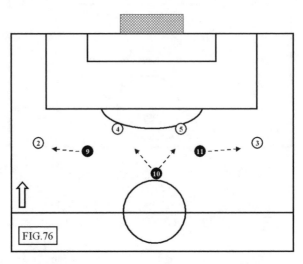

FIG.76

B. The three-quarter player lines up with the strikers on the weak side.

You still get offensive pressing, but the insertion now takes place on the weak side to give support to the pressure being brought to bear by the two strikers. This option is the most practical and realistic because when an attacking play is brought to an end you do not have the whole team already lined up in a block to defend itself.

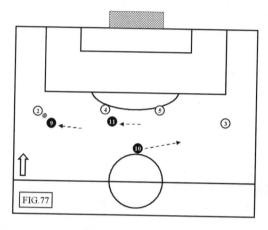

FIG.77

C. Three-quarter player moves back along the midfield line in the central zone.

This is a stand by attitude to play for time and cover the spaces. In this case the inside midfielders must be ready to shift outwards towards the flanks.

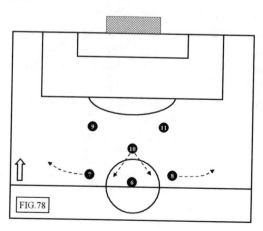

FIG.78

D. The three-quarter player moves back to the midfield on the weak side.

When the three-quarter player is not good at the defense phase, this solution allows him to move back to a part of the field that does not require him to do so quickly and urgently.
However, this type of solution can create a number of disadvantages. It becomes improbable that the team will regain possession immediately, and if the three-quarter player moves too far back he might not be effective in the development of the subsequent break.

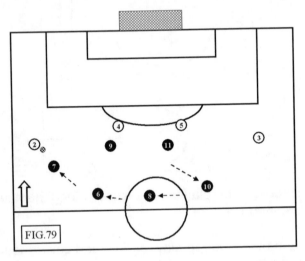

FIG.79

In the phase of non-possession the 4-3-1-2 has this disadvantage: if the three-quarter player does not participate in the defense phase - at least by covering the spaces - the team will usually find itself with only three players in the midfield. That will give them great difficulty in effectively covering the width of the opponents' playing front.
To get over this problem, we could simplify by saying that during the defense phase the team should get into formation as a 4-3-3 if you want them to regain possession in depth, or a 4-4-2 should you go for a stand by approach.

THE 3-5-2 / 5-3-2 SYSTEMS

In the phase of non-possession both the 3-5-2 and the 5-3-2 are systems that follow three-man defense principles, whether you are using zonal, man to man or man in zone defense.
Apart from looking at the attacking and defense mechanisms, we will also be making a rundown of the differences between the two systems.

PRINCIPLE CHARACTERISTICS OF THE 3-5-2 SYSTEM

Defense phase of the 3-5-2:

- With two strikers and all of five midfielders, pressing will be in the offensive zone.
- The side midfielder defending on the weak side will have to tighten the diagonal to form a four-man defense line.
- The defense position of the midfield playmaker with the three central midfielders. He will form a triangle with a low lying apex as far as the wings are concerned, and a rhombus with the three center defenders.
- If necessary the half wings will cover the side midfielders.

Attacking phase of the 3-5-2:

- The side midfielders look for depth and width, making movements without the ball.
- The strikers use cuts and dumps as attacking themes.
- The strikers cross over.
- The side midfielders use crosses as finishing touches.
- The midfield playmaker is always in support of the action by providing an outlet.
- The half wings make movements into space in support of the strikers.
- The center defenders open out when play is being built up to widen the playing front and cover the whole width of the field.

PRINCIPLE CHARACTERISTICS OF THE 5-3-2 SYSTEM

Defense phase of the 5-3-2

- Pressing is to be carried out in the defense zone.
- The defense line will always be made up of five players.
- The midfield playmaker positions himself to screen the defense.
- Priority in the defense zone to the two half-wings coming out to put pressure on the ball.
- In the defense zone the half wings will double up with the side midfielders.
- The three center defenders keep a central position (central concentration of the defense).

Attacking phase of the 5-3-2:

- The strikers use cuts, dump and rebounds and crossovers as their attacking themes.
- The half wings look for depth with movements without the ball above the side midfielders.
- The side midfielders look for width to widen out the attacking front during build up.
- The midfield playmaker supports the action to give outlet to the play.
- The first striker uses deviations and dumps with his head.

Differences in structuring schemes between the 3-5-2 and the 5-3-2:

What are the real differences that come up on the field?
What differences are there in the development of play and in the structure of the attack and the defense?

It will be immediately clear that:

- The 5-3-2 has a much lower center of balance because in has a 5-man defense line.
- The 5-3-2 will therefore opt for defense pressing and breaks to counter attack into space in the opponent's half.

- In the attacking phase, the 5-3-2 will be able to give width and depth to play with the disengagement of the two center half wings who will move to gain space above the side defenders (cf. Fig. 80).

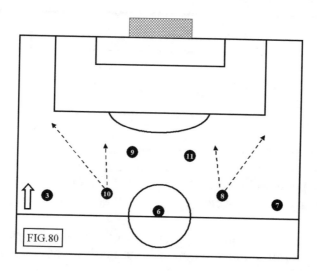

FIG.80

- In the attacking phase the 5-3-2 will develop play primarily with a central action made of short passes and dumps. The two strikers will make opposing movements and will act in such a way as to make use of the whole width of the field to become points of reference in attack and to give the team time to move up.
- In defense the 5-3-2 will have a five-man defense, which will give secure coverage. Depending on the position of the ball or on the coach's indications (fixed sweeper), one of the defenders will become the last man to cover.
- In the 5-3-2 during the defense phase with the ball on the flank and one of the side defenders moving out, the half wing will double up and the in depth coverage will be guaranteed by the central marker (cf. Fig. 81).

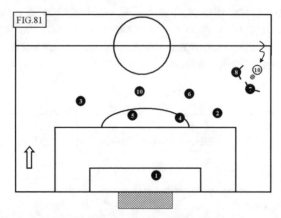

FIG.81

What makes the difference between the 3-5-2 and the preceding system of play is that the first has more attacking power and its center of balance is therefore higher, which means that it will be trying to regain possession in a more offensive zone of the field.

- In the 3-5-2 you foresee that the side midfielders give depth and width to attacking play, with the half wings tending to cover space.
- The 3-5-2 will try harder to get to the baseline and use the cross as its attacking theme.
- Even if they are acting right across the attacking front, the strikers will be nearer to each other and they will move in opposing directions.
- Because the side players are more in depth and in order not to unbalance the team even more, the half wings will move back if necessary during the defense phase to give coverage to the side midfielders (cf. Fig. 82).

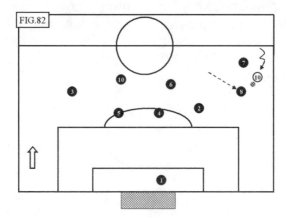

FIG.82

From what we have set out there are undeniable differences between the two systems. Sometimes, however, the contingent situations during the match or the characteristics of the players can lead to the adoption of one or the other of the two systems.

CHAPTER 4

PRINCIPLES OF PLAY

The last step of our long voyage is without doubt the most important, at least for those who believe (but even for those who do not) that it is the work you do on the field which determines the performance of the team.

The performance that a coach can expect from his team is strictly connected to the present or past coaching sessions, which means that he can only ask his players to do what he has prepared them to do.
Nothing more.

The coach must keep track of every single detail, from the particulars connected to the performance of the single player to those connected to the team in general.
If you improve the players and their individual qualities, you will get a corresponding upgrade in the global results.

The things to look after in the individual player are:

> · The psychological aspect.
> · The technical / tactical aspect.
> · The physical aspect.

From the specific technical / tactical point of view what the coach must pass on to every player are the techniques and know-how connected with all the various points of reference of play.
In other words:

> · The ball;
> · Space and time;
> · The teammates;
> · The opponents.

These other points of reference come out in training and during instruction:

> · Basic techniques.
> · The principles of individual tactics.
> · The principles of collective strategy.
> · The development of play.

Every player must be in possession of all these abilities and skills; and it is the coach's job to supply them.
It is only in this way that the player will be complete and able to express himself in a global - and therefore complicated - situation of play.

The first thing to see to in the individual is without doubt his basic techniques:

By basic techniques we mean the technical fundamentals of the game: to put it in a nutshell, the relationship between a soccer player and the ball.
In other words:

- Controlling the ball;
- Dribbling the ball;
- Kicking the ball;
- Receiving the ball;
- Heading the ball,
- Contrasting;
- Saving (the keeper).

The first and certainly the most important component in the game of soccer is the ball. It goes without saying that the players must have confidence with this instrument, and their self-assurance must be developed and expanded at every age and at every level.
The greater the player's technical ability, the more the coach will be able to ask from him on the field, putting forward more and more complicated solutions.

If the player knows how to kick the ball he will be better able to hit the goal when shooting or carry out a fast, precise pass when building up play ...
First of all, the relationship with the ball.

The next step along the formative process that a player must get on top of if he wants to be able to resolve the problems that come up in every situation of play are those connected with his knowledge of the principles of individual tactics.

What we are talking about here is an application of basic techniques in a simple situation of play (against a single opponent): applied techniques or individual tactics.
The relationship between a soccer player and his opponent.

Principles of individual tactics

POSSESSION PHASE	NON-POSSESSION PHASE
Getting free of marking	Taking up position
Defending and covering the ball	Marking
Passing	Contrasting
Dummies / dribbling	Intercepting
Shooting	Defending the goal

These are the principles in the two phases of play and you can start by looking at them in a simple situation of play, 1 against 1 with the ball or 1 against 1 away from the ball.

From a simple situation you move on to a more complex one concerning more than two players. At this point we start talking about collective tactics, in other words, coordinated and collaborative play between two or more players.
The relationship between a player and a teammate.

To set it out schematically:

Principles of collective tactics

POSSESSION PHASE	NON-POSSESSION PHASE
Ranking	Ranking (coverage)
Depth	Delaying action
Width	Concentration
Mobility	Balance
Unpredictability	Control

These are the principles that the players will have to follow during the two phases of play in complicated 2 against 1, 2 against 2 etc.

Apart from schemes and tables, what the coach has to train are the principles of play in all possible situations, from the simplest ones to the most complicated during the two phases of play (possession and non-possession), with the ball and without the ball, near the ball and far away from the ball.
These are the indispensable basics that make it possible to develop such principles on the field in a clear strategy of play. Putting these principles into action is called the development of play.

The development of play

POSSESSION PHASE	NON-POSSESSION PHASE
One / two	Pressing
One / three	Double teaming
Cuts	Offside
Dump and rebounds	
Feints (fakes)	
Overlapping	
Change of play	
Possession	
Numerical superiority	
Crossovers	

These developments of play are the means with which every player and every team attempts to carry out its play.

Every player must be in full possession of all these skills (and principles of play) in order to be able to follow the coach's instructions and put forward team play.

The coach's job, above all at the youth level, is to give instructions on how to put them into effect.

When he comes out of the youth sector, a young player will have to know the game of soccer and have the means (physical and technical ability and tactical principles) to allow him to use these skills.

Basic techniques and knowledge of the principles of the game - these take priority when giving instruction at the youth level.

4.1 Making progress

When we begin to speak of the tactical organization of teams, we are obviously directing our attention towards coaches that are working with players who are already skilled or who are in any case well on the way to being so: that is, to coaches of first teams or, in certain circumstances and then only in relation to special skills, to coaches of the more advanced junior teams (though be careful even here!).

We will now have a look at the various methods that can be put into effect, the planning, the sequence of work, and then we will move on to the field itself (grass and mud, sweat and exertion) to put forward some ideas.

You will understand, first of all, that the team must be organized in each phase of play and in every zone of the field, and so we will have to give coaching in the following situations:

POSSESSION PHASE	NON-POSSESSION PHASE
Defensive half of the field	Defensive half of the field
Midfield	Midfield
Attacking half of the field	Attacking half of the field

The team's tactical organization will have to be built up keeping in mind the phases of play (possession or non-possession) and the zone of the field in which the attacking or defending play is developing (defensive half of the field, midfield or attacking half of the field).

These are the first points of reference to keep in mind when building up the team from a tactical point of view.

At this point you have to decide what playing phase and which level of the field to start from.

This is a choice the coach will have to make depending on the necessities or the peculiarities of his team, or, even better, of the characteristics of the game which he most wishes to underline.

For example, a team that wishes to make possession of the ball its principle characteristic will begin with the attacking phase, while a team that wants to concentrate on breaking back into play will start by working on the defense phase. Of course, there is nothing rigid about all this; it is only an indication about the tendency of your work and of the play you will be putting on show on the field.

Decisions like these may seem almost marginal, but they can become important when giving character to the team and as indications of the mentality and the strategy of play that you wish to set up.

During the first days of work (which are the most important from a psychological point of view), the coach must be able to get his own beliefs across - his personal ideas about soccer.

He must impress things in a lasting way on the minds of his players, giving them razor-sharp instructions on how they will be working and on what will be expected of them.

You can decide to start from the non-possession or from the possession phase, or you can blend the two areas of work, giving equal space to the two phases. Work usually begins on the defense phase, even if the present writer believes that, if you want to propose this type of tactical work, above all with young players, it might be better to begin with the attacking phase because this will stimulate and induce the players to think more about actually building up play rather than just destroying it.

Apart from the phase of play which you decide to start off from, we believe that the midfield is the best zone from which to develop the team's mechanisms of play. From there you can decide to go on to the attacking half or the defending half depending on your particular needs and / or preferences.

To sum up the sequence of work:

DEFENSE OR ATTACKING PHASE

MIDFIELD

DEFENSIVE OR ATTACKING HALF OF THE FIELD

The important thing, in any case, is that you organize the team while always keeping in mind these first points of reference.

The next step is to associate the two phases of play to make the situation on the field more complete and realistic.
What we are talking about here is how to develop attacking play starting off from regaining possession or how to organize the defensive set up when the team loses possession.
This is to underline the transition between one phase and the other and the concept by which:

> · The team that is attacking starts to defend;
> · The team that is defending starts to organize attacking play.

Examples:

The team is building up play on the left flank, the side back detaching himself from his line. The remaining three defenders shift onto the strong side to cover the zone left unattended, with one or two defenders on the opposing strikers and a defender covering depth.

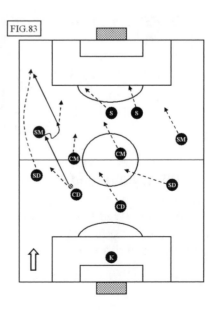

FIG.83

Again: having lost possession the team moves back in order to absorb the opponents' play. While this is going on, the striker returning to shorten up space will position himself on the weak side (defending against a possible change of play) so that he will be ready for a change of front in the next attacking move.

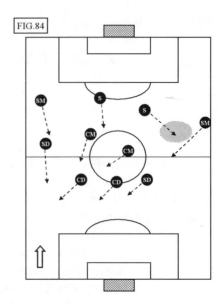

These are the first points of reference to work on in order to get full tactical organization.

Here is a rundown of the progress of work:

POSSESSION and NON-POSSESSION PHASE

MIDFIELD

DEFENSIVE and ATTACKING HALVES OF THE FIELD

REGAINING THE BALL and LOSING THE BALL

THE MIDFIELD

DEFENSIVE and ATTACKING HALVES OF THE FIELD

We will now have a look at the various operative means to be used - the various methods that can be applied to the tactical operations of the team.

4.2 Methods

What should we do on the field and what methods should we use?

Our aim is to organize the team from a tactical point of view. Leaving the details to one side, we will be considering global methods of intervention with exercises on the tactical construction of the team.

Every coaching session must have an objective, both on the technical and the physical level, and also as far as individual and / or collective tactics are concerned.

These objectives must be interconnected in the same session or during the weekly program to create a one track line of conduct.

In the week's program the coach will have to consider and set objectives in the following areas:

- Basic techniques (present in every session):
- Principles of individual tactics in defense and in attack;
- Principles of collective tactics in defense and in attack;
- Tactical organization of the team in the phase of non-possession;
- Developing play in the attacking phase connected with the system of play and the strategies adopted;
- Dead balls in the defense and the attacking phase;
- Athletic preparation (present in every session);
- Psychological preparation for the match (present in every session).

Your program will depend on a number of variables: the number of training sessions, the space you have on hand, the level of the players you are coaching, the climate ... - and, naturally, the aims you have set down for yourself.

The makeup of the training session will naturally depend on your objectives. If you want it to be all-encompassing and truly instructive from every point of view, it will have to include three different approaches to the targets you wish to reach:

· Generic approach;
· Thematic approach;
· Situational approach.

The generic approach is when you do exercises that have no precise points of reference (i.e., ball possession in a square). The thematic approach is when you play a training match going for an attacking or defensive theme. The situational approach is when you are trying to copy what happens during a game, with reference to space and time as in match conditions.

For example, if the main point of the session is the development of overlapping as an attacking play:

==>   Generic approach: ball possession in a square continually attempting to get two or three (one / three) players to overlap (give and go above the ball).
==>   Thematic approach: a match on a reduced field where the goal will be valid only after overlapping on the flanks between side players.
==>   Situational approach: attack against defense (6 against 5 in one half of the field using your own system in attack and the system employed by the next opponents in defense, goals being valid only after overlapping on the flanks.

What operative methods should be used in order to give global tactical organization to the team?

Once we have underlined the fact that to get good team organization (and the right response from the players in carrying out what has been suggested to them), it is necessary to pay particular attention to details, giving the players the know-how and the critical ability to choose. We will then concentrate on the methods to be used and the operative means that will allow us to work on the global aspect.

The methods and the operative means allowing us to reach our final goal - the tactical construction of the team - will be based on collective tactics for the team as a whole and for single sections both in the possession and in the non-possession phase.

OPERATIVE MEANS:

DEFENSE PHASE	ATTACKING PHASE
Movements of approach	'Shadow' match, 11 against 0
Defense shifts	Match using attacking themes
Attack against defense	Attack against defense
Match in numerical inferiority / superiority	Match in numerical inferiority / superiority
Match using defense themes	Match using defense themes
Match, 11 against 11	Match, 11 against 11

In the next section we will be going into details, having a close look at each operative method, keeping in mind how to build up the work and illustrating some examples of exercises as ideas.

4.3 EXERCISES

We are now at the last step - the most practical and therefore the most important one.
We will be having an in-depth look at all the operative means, suggesting a number of exercises that the coach can use to train and construct a team from a tactical point of view.
We feel that when working with young players the most suitable operative means are those that allow them to acquire experience and tactical principles during play.
In this sense the best exercises are theme matches or pitting the attack against the defense (in numerical equality, superiority or inferiority).

The first thing we would like to look at is how to coach movements of approach, i.e., in those factors that set down the team's movements during the various phases of play.
Basically, we will have to remember:

· The team that is attacking tends to lengthen and widen itself out;
· The team that is defending tends to shorten up and tighten in.

When receiving tactical instruction, the players have to learn how to open out and close in.

Movements of approach.

The team is lined up in and around the midfield using its own system (in this case, the 4-3-3); when the coach gives the signal it will carrying out successive opening out movements (ball to its own keeper so that he can come out with his hands) or those connected with closing in (ball to the opponents' keeper for clearing with foot or hand).

Opening out movements (Fig. 85)

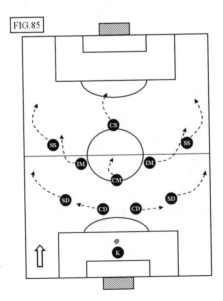

Closing in movements (Fig. 86).

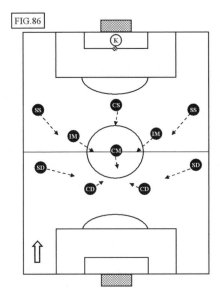

Movements to open out towards the right (cf. Fig. 87).

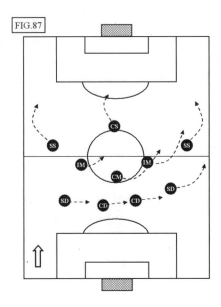

The next step is to carry out opening movements towards the right or left when you think the keeper will come out with his hands.

We will then continue by concentrating on the defense phase, i.e., with the opponents in possession.

To make it easier, we will call these movements 'defensive shifts'.

As we have already said, it is important to carry out shifts in all zones of the field: in the attacking half, in the defending half and in the central zone.
We advise starting off the work in or around the midfield.
You will want to consider one or two conditions for this type of work.

> · How many players you have on hand;
> · How much space you have.

Defensive shifts on ten fixed artificial points of reference.

The team is lined up with its own system, and you set out ten fixed points of reference (cones, poles, colored flags …) in or around the midfield and organized depending on your needs (e.g., with the system used by your next opponent).
Each point of reference will have a color or a number allocated to it, and when the coach gives the signal the player whose job it is to mark the point of reference that has been called will come up to put it under pressure, imagining that it is an opponent in possession.

It follows that the whole team will get into position with that defensive point of reference using shifts and giving coverage.

Example: the 4-3-3 against the 4-4-2 (Fig. 88):

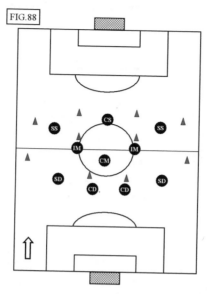

Shift on the defensive point of reference shown in Fig. 89 as number 3.

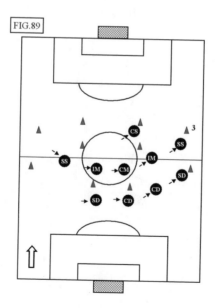

The same exercise should be done in different parts of the field to refine the routine defensive moves of the various sections of the team.

In-depth defensive shifts, again with the 4-3-3 against the 4-4-2 (Fig. 90).

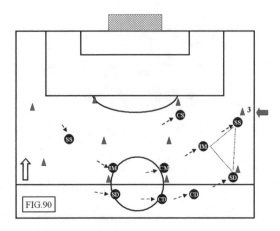

Defensive shifts at the back (Fig. 91).

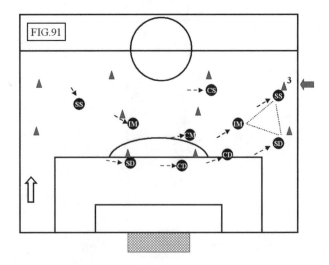

To complicate the exercise, the coach can change the timing of the signal. He can call out the new point of reference in the following moments:

· When the whole team is lined up to defend;
· When only the player who has come up in pressure is on the point of reference;
· When not even the player who is to come up has actually arrived on the point of reference.

This will make the team's shifts more difficult: by reducing the time between one signal and another you will be speeding up the play.

Defensive shifts on the 'chessboard'.

The chessboard is when you place more than ten fixed points of reference (cones, poles …) on the field so that each player will have more than one position to put pressure on. This will increase the variability of the exercise and make it more similar to a match. You usually place these points of reference to form squares so that each player will be able to come out in four different directions, forwards or backwards in the vertical sense, and towards the center or towards the sidelines in the horizontal. Once again, this exercise should be carried out in different parts of the field.

Example: you line the team up with its system (4-4-2) in or around the midfield.
The coach calls out the points of reference in succession, on which the nearest player comes up in pressure, and the rest of the team reacts with the relative shifts and covering moves (Fig. 92).

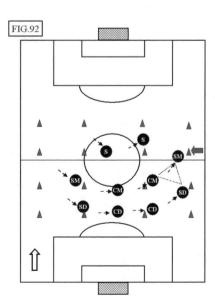

FIG.92

Defensive shifts on mobile points of reference

The following exercise follows the same concept, but instead of the fixed points of reference, we have a mobile one - the ball, put in movement by the coach.

The coach places himself in the center of the field and sends in a ball, which becomes the defense point of reference; a player will move in to stop it and the whole team will carry out the relative shifts.

After this the ball will be returned to the coach, who will then kick it into another zone so that the team can shift onto the new point of reference.

Either that or the coach will put a new ball on the field.

The team will carry out defensive or offensive pressing depending on the zone into which the coach kicks the ball (Fig. 93)

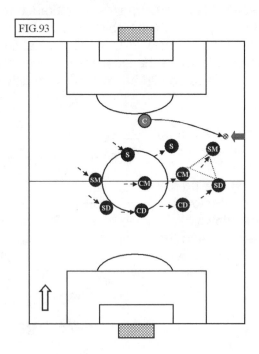

FIG.93

These exercises are good for those who do not have enough players on hand to create a real situation of play, and who cannot, therefore, field some players as opponents who will play the ball. Ten players are enough here, and where you do have a few extras, you make them play in pairs so that you can carry out the described exercises in any case.

You can make a working plan, starting off with each separate section.

· Only the defense;
· Only the midfield;
· Only the attack.

You will then go on to two sections together, finally fielding the whole team.

Some examples of sequence:

· Only the defense.
· Defense + midfield.
· The whole team.

Or:

· Only the attack
· Attack + midfield.
· The whole team.

The defect of defense exercises on fixed points of reference is that you get an artificial situation of play and cannot reflect the real conditions.

One or two important elements are missing:

· Timing the movement out to bring pressure to bear.
· Reading the ball (covered or uncovered ball).
· The opponents' supporting players.

You can resolve this in part and create more realistic situations of play by using players pretending to be opponents in possession as the points of reference

If you have twenty players you can field two teams choosing your playing systems (with one of the two working as the opponents in possession).

Examples of how to order the work:

You line up two teams in or around the midfield. The opposing team passes the ball around with their hands, and the other reacts to the position of the ball by bringing a player onto the opponent in possession and carrying out the relative shifts and giving coverage. You then start playing with feet but keeping the ball low and to the nearby supporting players, after which you can play with high balls to the supporting players.

To begin, the opponents will be placed in their respective zones of competence and they will then begin to change places with each other, keeping possession without finalizing play. The defending team will try to keep a player on the ball and maintain the correct distances in coverage.
The coach could instruct one of them to let the opponent dribble past so that the covering players can simulate closing in.

As you make progress, you should introduce the idea of the cov-ered / uncovered ball, getting the defending team to take up an attitude that can be more (or less) aggressive.
You play for time on an uncovered ball (unless you find yourself in a desperate situation of clear numerical inferiority); you attack a covered ball.
However, in a match the tactical situation is not always so plain, and that makes it difficult to read the ball situation correctly and to react to it. This is the real problem.
Also when scheduling this type of work, you will have to distin-guish the zone of field (the attacking half, the midfield and the defending half) when starting out, and the speed of the passes as well (going from slow to those that reflect the real situation).

The more players you have on hand, the more true to life the exercise and all its parts will be - timing the moves, space, reading the ball and marking the supporting players will all be addressed.

You can get a good result even without the help of all the players. You can eliminate some of the players in each section; or you can eliminate a whole section both for the team in possession and for the main team training in the defense phase.

Example 10 against 10.

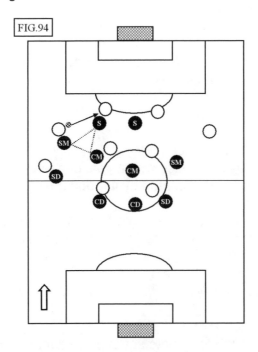

Two teams are lined up in and around the midfield, the main team with their own system and the other with the system to be used by the next opponent.
The team in possession keeps the ball in a static way.
The passes are carried out to the nearest supporting players after the opposing team have placed themselves with their relative coverage.
You then start to accelerate the movement of the ball, making it possible to pass to teammates further away.

You move on (ball possession becoming dynamic but without shooting on goal) with the defending team having to react to the position of the ball and the opponents' movements and carrying out the necessary coverage and also (if need be) exchanges of marking.

You can extend things to various parts of the field, playing in both the defense and the attacking zones.

Possession can be carried out giving preference to attacking themes that are typical of the team we are to face (e.g., if our next opponents make great use of overlapping to develop their play, then we will concentrate on this).

The exercise will finish off with finalized dynamic possession, i.e., by giving the opponents the chance to shoot.

Each play will end when:

> · The ball goes out of play.
> · The play concludes with a goal or a save.
> · The ball is intercepted by the defenders.

Each time the action ends, you start off again with the keeper or a defender putting the ball back into play, a pass deliberately mistaken by a defender after a series of passes or with the coach putting a new ball on the field.
In the exercises to follow we will be moving on to the attacking phase.

If you do not have a complete set of players for two teams, you can carry out the same exercise by eliminating a couple of players from each section of the opponents' team (i.e., the 4-4-1 or the 3-4-2 instead of the 4-4-2).

You could also use the players only as points of reference in width or in depth.

Example: you place the players as points of reference in different lines with a player or the coach in the middle to keep the ball moving.

Whoever is in possession becomes the point of reference for the defense.
Later on, the player in possession can bring the ball forward a meter or two (uncovered ball) or bring it backward (covered ball) with the team reacting correctly.

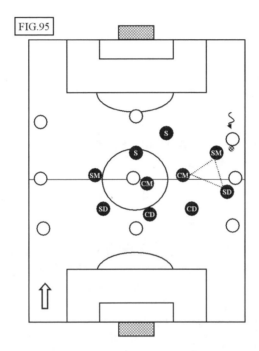

FIG.95

You can also work on the sections, lining up your defense + midfield against an opposing attack and midfield.
Example: the 3-4-3 against the 4-4-2. You line up a 3-4 against a 4-2 (you can add the opposing side defenders to put the defense in difficulty).
The three-man defense is usually coached using the midfield as well, or at least its side players.
You can carry out the exercise in the defense or midfield zone and you move on with the work as in the preceding examples, i.e., you start off with a passive attitude, becoming semi-active and then moving on to a real playing situation. (Fig. 96)

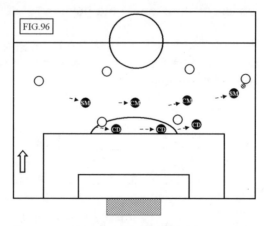

You can also line up your attack + midfield against opposing defense and midfield.

Example of a 3-4-3 against a 4-4-2: you line up a 3-4 against a 4-4 in the attacking zone.

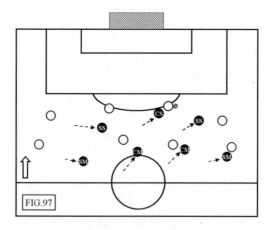

As you can see there are innumerable possibilities.
In the exercises above we have been looking at the defense phase and so the coach's attention and the priorities of the training session are directed towards the phase of non-possession. We will never tire of saying that all these exercises - above all when we are talking about young players - are to be carried out when all the principles of marking have been consolidated or, in any case, inserted in a schedule that has as its principle objective

instruction on the principles of play - in this case of course concerning defense.

We will now move on to the attacking phase - the moment when our team is in possession.
The most widely used operative method, above all at the beginning of the schedule of work, is without any doubt the shadow match, 11 against 0.
When you want to work on any particular aspect you should come up with a method and a practical situation that underlines its features.
When talking about the attacking phase, playing against no opposition will give the greatest possible advantage to your team.
There are many ways of doing this type of work, but the important thing is to get things right step by step so that you finish up knowing how to carry out the proposed attacking themes in a real situation of play.

The basic concept of the 11 against 0 is that the repetition of the movements will allow the players to learn them by heart.

This does not mean, however, that we will produce real play only through this type of work - quite the contrary.
It is above all through our preliminary preparations running up to this that we give the necessary information to arrive at good attacking themes.
For example: if you wish to make great use of overlapping as an attacking theme, you must not limit yourself to carrying it out in the shadow match, but it must be brought up in theme matches, with exercises on using two men to break free of marking, 2 against 1 situations of play, overlapping, etc.
Only in this way will the players be able to learn how and when to carry it out during a match in real and complex situations.
We make the mechanisms automatic by repeating the 11 against 0.

In itself the 11 against 0 is a completely unreal situation except as far as the size of the field is concerned and in the number of team members.
It becomes necessary, therefore, to bring in some adjustments in

order to make the situation just a little more realistic.
We will do this by introducing a number of playing 'conditions'.

We will call the next exercises the 'Conditioned 11 against 0'.

The first thing we need to condition is the starting point, i.e., the part of the field from which you begin your attacking play.

As in the defense phase, you have to work in all parts of the field:

> · Starting off in the defensive half of the field;
> · Starting off in the midfield area;
> · Starting off in the attacking zone.

By conditioning the starting off point of play, and therefore of the ball, you are also conditioning the placement of the players going into action; so, if we are beginning from the defensive half of the field all the players will be crushed into the lower half, while if we regain possession in the midfield, the players will be in and around the halfway line and if we regain the ball in depth the players will be in the attacking zone.

As for the schedule regarding the defense phase, we think it better here as well to begin from the midfield.

When you have conditioned the starting off point of the ball and therefore of the players, you need to condition the play or plays that bring the team to shooting at goal, giving priority plays for each zone of the field and each single situation.

Next, you condition the timing of the plays, changing the number of touches allowed to teach the players how to time their break into action.
You can do this by asking the players to use two touch play (not one and not three!), or three touch plays, only one touch being allowed on a backward pass, and so on.
You can also use markers (poles or cones) to indicate the timing and the space of the passes, changes of speed, running with the ball or changes of direction.
The last thing you condition is the point of arrival, for example a

square or a cone into or beyond which the ball has to arrive
before the shot on goal.

To sum up:

> · Condition the starting off point;
> · Condition the plays;
> · Condition time;
> · Condition the point of arrival.

When actually carrying out the exercise, you can decide not to
use all four of the conditions at the same time, but to introduce
them one or two at a time.

Examples of a conditioned 11 against 0:

3-4-3 against 0.

2 brings the ball to a marker cone, and, being closed in at this
point, makes a long pass to 9, who has in the meantime length-
ened out. He makes a dump on 7's cut under him, and 7
rebounds filtering the ball into space for 11, who shoots beyond a
cone placed just outside the area.

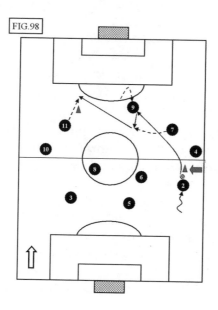

FIG.98

Or:

4-3-3 against 0

Obligatory two touch play after a compulsory one touch dump. The defense having passed the ball along the line, 2 plays onto 7's inward cut; 7 dumps on his supporting player 6, who sends the ball directly to 8 as he breaks free of marking into depth in the space marked out by a square.

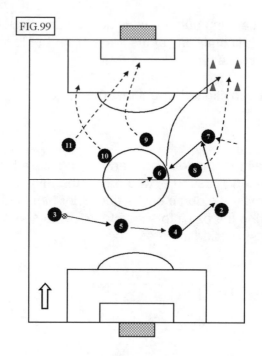

FIG.99

As he progresses with his schedule, the coach will have to map out this kind of work, and that is possible if he conditions the players' movements by creating artificial situations of play.

When the players have assimilated these exercises and the coach has put forward various different movements, you can then move on to a different type of 11 against 0.

11 against 0 exercises with an attacking theme.

In this type of shadow match you do not condition the plays, but ask the players to develop a particular attacking theme during the offensive action.

Example: shooting on goal after overlapping on the flanks.
The coach will put a ball into play in whatever part of the field he wants, and the team must get a shot on goal by overlapping.

4-4-2 against 0.

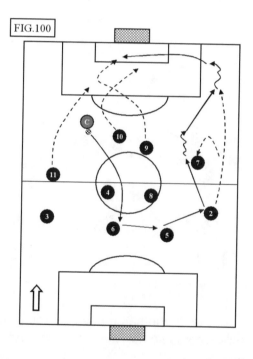

FIG.100

2 plays the ball on 7's move to meet him, and then overlaps him on the outside.
Now free, 7 makes for the goal and gets the ball to 2 (who has attacked space from the outside) for the cross. Naturally, there are a great number of possibilities, and you can connect two attacking themes in the same action.

Example: change of play + one / two:

4-3-3 against 0.

Having received the ball, 7 is closed off and dumps on his supporting player 6; he changes play for 10, who in the meantime has opened himself up on the weak side.
10 makes for the center and shoots after having carried out a one / two with eleven.

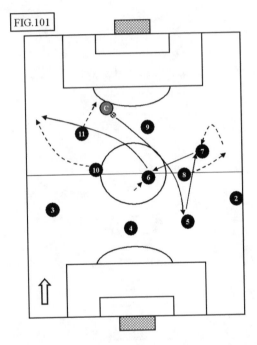

FIG.101

It is very important that in the same session you repeatedly try out just a few movements so that the exercises get their point home to the players.
To repeat: try out at the most two movements in the same session!

You can connect the attacking theme of the 11 against 0 to an exercise on defensive shifts. In this way you move from defense to an attacking play.
Once again, this type of work is to be carried out on three levels of the field.

Example: passing from the defense to the attacking phase.

The team lines up with their system; the coach then puts a ball onto the field, which becomes the point of reference onto which a player will have to 'come out', the rest of the team consolidates by making connected shifts and moves to give coverage.
When they are in position, the player in possession sets off with the ball for conditioned or unconditioned attacking play.

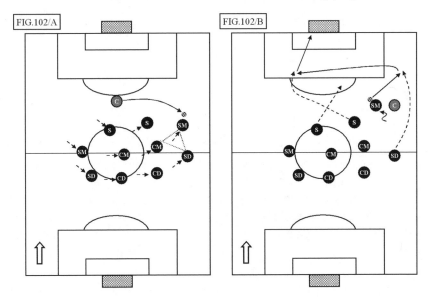

Or: passing from the attacking to the defending phase.

Fielded in its own system, the team develops a conditioned or unconditioned attacking play; at the coach's signal the ball becomes the opposing point of reference and the team forms the defensive block.

In this type of exercise you are concentrating on the attitude when the team moves from one phase to another in a dynamic situation, with defenders that might be moving into attack just when possession is lost and attacking players moving back into defense the moment possession is regained.

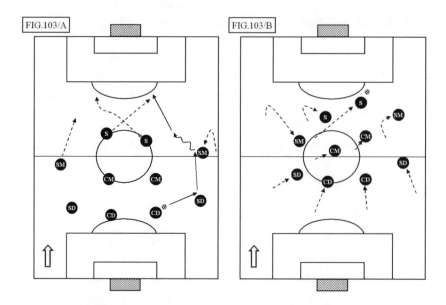

After having worked on situations where the two phases of play are being coached in separate moments, or rather, where they are being coached without the presence of opponents in order to make it easier for the players to grasp the concepts, we must then move on to 'all-encompassing' work, in which the two phases are trained at the same time in the presence of opponents.

At this point, then, we are giving instruction on the attacking and defense phases in situations of play in the presence of active opponents. Real play. The match.

The most effective operative instrument is without doubt the 'theme' match, i.e., a match where you pay particular attention to a single concept to be developed and coached.
There are three types of 'theme' matches:

> · Attack against defense theme match
> · Attacking or defense theme match
> · Numerical superiority / inferiority match.

Attack against defense matches work very well in training because they reproduce real-life situations (even if with a reduced number of players) in that the special references - i.e., the size of the field - are the same as during a match.

It is important to underline the objective of the training session and to organize the exercise to make sure you are paying specific attention to coaching the attacking phase or the defense phase.

The length of the field will depend on the number of players involved in the exercise and on the tactical and conditional objective decided upon. If your objective is the attacking phase, you need to:

- · Line the players up in their usual system;
- · Line up the defenders in the system used by the opponents;
- · Create playing situations on different levels of the field;
- · Perhaps give the attacking players numerical superiority;
- · Get the defenders to start off with a passive attitude.

Example: 6 against 5 to shoot on goal in the attacking phase.

4-2 in attack against 4-1 in defense.

You are playing in the attacking half of the field to finalize play. The two center midfielders in attack use maximum two touch play and only in support of the action.
When the defenders have regained possession, a center midfielder restarts play on the halfway line.

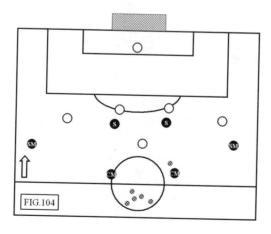

FIG.104

6 against 6 to build up in the attacking phase.

You play in the defense half of the field to coach the build up action.
The aim of the player in possession is to bring the ball into a touchdown area placed at the halfway line, or, alternatively, to score in the goals positioned there while being disturbed by the opponents' pressing.

Field with the touchdown area (Fig. 105).

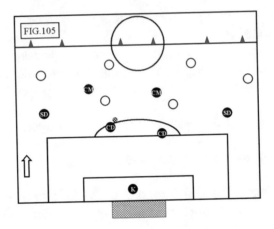

Field with goals (Fig. 106).

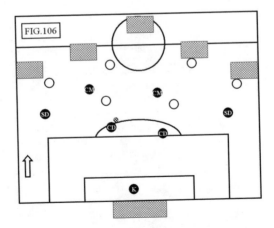

8 against 6 in the central zone for finishing touches.

You play in or around the halfway line and the defenders are not allowed to move out of that area.

The aim of the attacking players is to score goals by filtering a ball over the line on the three quarter field without it being intercepted.

The conclusive part of the play is carried out at maximum speed without the defenders disturbing the action.

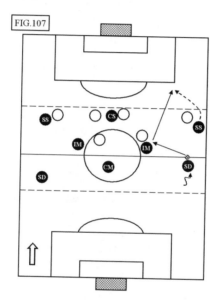

FIG.107

To put the attacking players at an advantage, all these exercises can be carried out with the defenders initially keeping to a semi-passive attitude, i.e., staying in position without touching the ball and not representing a real obstacle.

If you want to concentrate on the defense phase you will need to:

- Line the players up in their own system;
- Line up the opponents in your next opponent's system;
- Work on different levels of the field;
- Keep the defenders in numerical inferiority or equality;
- Have the attacking players in initial static possession or without shooting on goal.

6 against 6 defending 4 goals or four touchdown areas for the opposing attacking action.

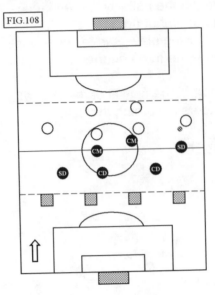

Variant with eight goals: you defend and attack four goals.

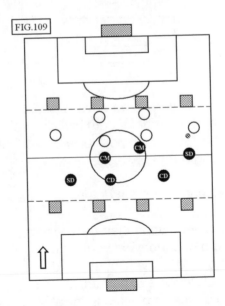

When we talk about goals or touchdown areas we are talking about two different concepts. If I have to defend or attack a touchdown area, I will have to disengage myself into a space (the area in question) if I am attacking; if I am defending, I must absorb an attack without the ball or a striking run with the ball. When we are playing with the goals, I will have to shoot or pass the ball into the net if I am attacking; and if I am defending I will have to try to intercept the ball by defending the line of the pass.

Naturally, the exercises given as examples for the attacking phase are valid also for the defense phase, though in that case the coach will reverse his point of view and what he is concentrating on.
It is easy to see that in a real situation of play the phase of possession and non-possession inevitably get mingled up and sessions like these without the coach giving any particular directives will end up coaching both phases.

Particular attacking or defense themes can be interwoven into these kinds of matches.

If you want to develop overlapping during the attacking phase, you will play a 6 against 5 or an 8 against 6 with corridors on the flanks, making side overlapping an requirement before shooting.

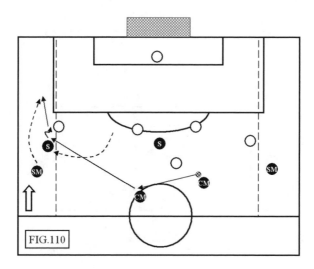

FIG.110

If you want to concentrate on cuts, you come up with a match forcing the players to cut in on a filtered pass to a touchdown area on the three quarter line.

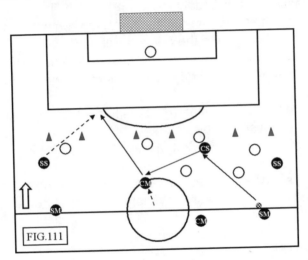

FIG.111

You can coach defense themes - offside tactics, for example - in a match with the systematic application of offside or putting pressure on the opponents' back passes or on their pressing, with the defense line coming into depth when the keeper kicks back into play or with a player on an opponent.

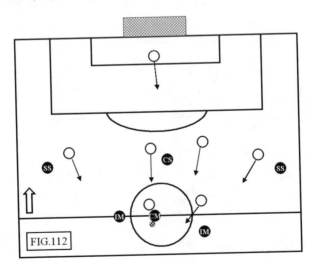

FIG.112

11 against 5 or 11 against 6.

A good way of working on a particular attacking theme is the attacking players against defense match, with the attacking players in strong numerical superiority. You line up your 'first choice' players in a part of the field and in their system against a few opponents placed here and there on the three lines of play, who will be creating obstacles to the offensive action.

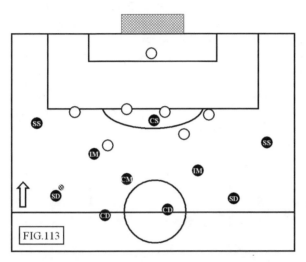

FIG.113

The best coaching method is probably - no, definitely - 11 against 11 exercises because they contain all the points of reference (numbers, space and timing) that come up during a match, bringing the simulation very close to what will actually be happening on the field.
Once again there are, of course, numerous situations that the coach can invent depending on the objectives he has in mind.

Possible ideas:

- · Number of touches in each team section;
- · Number of touches in the zones of the field (attacking, central and defense);
- · Number of touches in each vertical sector (side or central chains);
- · Required passes in sequence between team sections with different colored vests;

· Back or forward balls;
· Low balls,
· Semi-passive attitude of the defenders, who are therefore only in position;
· Dribbling forbidden in certain parts of the field and defense allowed only to intercept;
· Attacking and defending team keep possession without finalizing;
· Obligatory development of certain particular attacking or defending themes;
· Corridors or lines marking out touchdown areas in which the attacking action is to be carried out;
· Match in or around the half way line defending touch down areas or goals, which will then give freedom to the opponents' attacking play or allow it to be contrasted by only a few defenders.

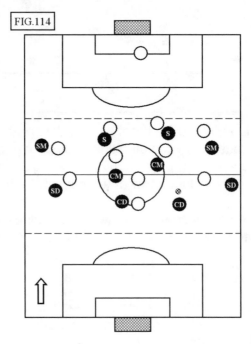

FIG.114

There are innumerable possibilities, and the coach can use his imagination and creativity to come up with the right exercises to reach the objectives he has set.

Methods of training on dead balls are a separate question, and they, too, have become fundamental to the tactical set up of a team both in attack and in defense because many goals are scored in this way.

Without looking at how they are to be kicked, we will make a run-down of how to program the work to be carried out.

Sequence of work in coaching on dead balls.

The defense phase:

- The opponents' keeper putting the ball back into play;
- Your own keeper putting the ball back into play;
- Corner kicks;
- Side free kicks;
- Free kicks from the defense three quarter;
- Throw in (attacking, defense and central zone);
- Penalties;
- Free kicks near the goal
- Opponents' kick off (hoping they will be doing it as often as possible!).

Attacking phase:

- Kick off;
- Keeper putting the ball back into play;
- Direct or indirect free kicks from near the goal,
- Side free kicks and those on the opponent's three quarter;
- Penalties;
- Corner kicks;
- Throw in (defense, attacking and central zones).

Sequence of work:

- Without opponents;
- Against passive opponents - only in position;
- Against a few active opponents;
- Against active opponents.

All these things can be tried out on their own and in succession, or they can be inserted in a theme match whose focus will be dead balls. For example, you play an attack against defense starting off with a free kick; you play on for a minute or two or until the end of the action and then start again with another free kick.

Do not underestimate the work to be done on the throw in because there will be many of these during a match. To coach them in the attacking phase you can follow this progression:

- Without opponents.
- Passive opponents.
- A few active opponents.
- Against active opponents, who will not oppose the opening move.
- Against opponents who are always active.

You can get to work using the 11 against 0 and starting off with the throw in or with theme matches beginning play from a throw in.
It is important that you coach both phases of play in all three zones of the field.

4.4 Notes and ideas

It goes without saying that these are not the only coaching methods useful for building up the team from a tactical point of view. You need to apply a global approach which will include all aspects of the game - psychological, technical, tactical and physical.
What the team does on the field is the fruit of the work that has been carried out during coaching sessions.

It is true, of course that the players are the ones who play the game, but there is no doubt that a good coach and the first-rate work done by the technical staff can really make the difference.

We have not tried to put across revolutionary ideas or magic formulas, but we know that a working plan, its step by step progression and its basic quality are all aspects that are far from being insignificant.
You must know what to do and how to do it.
The principles of soccer, the basic rules and the principles of marking and getting free of marking are all things that have not changed with the passing of time; but training methods have changed and will surely continue to do so.

The strategic objective of this book was to give a study and working plan that will help in the tactical construction of a soccer team.
Our teaching aim was to have supplied you with some ideas which can at least be discussed and in which you will I hope find inspiration.
Putting you in a position to think and talk about soccer in a different way.

Conclusions

Regrettably, or fortunately, I am not very good at finishing off; not a day passes, and every time I read or re-read these pages I get a new idea, yet another inspiration. But I am like that, with my unending desire to develop, to discover new worlds and different things, to put myself in question - and this book should be read and interpreted in that way: as a discussion and with great critical spirit. Take these pages as jumping off points from which you can bring back new and perhaps interesting ideas that will be useful to your work and your experience.

They are nothing more than simple, practical examples to whet your appetite for the study of this subject, which in itself is as interesting as it is enigmatic - and which has its bizarre side as well.

I strongly believe that the practice of this sport is fundamentally based on training methods.

I believe that the match is but the fruit and the mirror image of the week's work, and that you must always broaden your horizons of study so that the level of play goes higher and higher.

We study things to make them better, and soccer methods are no exception.

Basic to any kind of improvement is to put yourself in question, to open your mind towards the new and also the old, not to close up in irremovable dogma - and it is that which allows us to develop, and with us soccer as well.

It has been said that soccer methods are an 'inexact science', and that beyond everything and everybody we are at the mercy of a ball that goes in or a ball that comes out, of a clump of grass, of a sunny day or a day of rain. I reply that we must believe in something.

Always.

Believe and try to improve.

And that is true because when all is said and done soccer is not only a simple statistic, a detached number - it is also a question of people's feelings.

You have to play in a way that will bring out those feelings; you have to coach your team to bring out those feelings.

To those that say you must get results, I reply that we must also give emotions.
In the end it is not he who works, but he who works better that goes to the top - by which I do not mean that he will be the winner.
It happens.

I would like to thank:

We have arrived to the end of this long journey and I hope I have
not lost anybody on the way. A great number of people have
made this book possible, in different ways for different reasons
and at different times, all of them important; people without whom
I would not have been able to carry out this long and difficult but
at the same time exhilarating task which may have had soccer as
its principle subject, but that was not the only thing I had to relate
to as I got down to work.

As far as I am concerned at least, writing sucks you into a completely different dimension, it takes away time and energy. There
are days when you cannot put down a word, and others when
dawn breaks and you are still at the keyboard; and while you are
living your normal life you lose yourself in thoughts about what
you can or would like to write. Inspiration comes to you and if you
can't take it on the wing it escapes you again and will not come
back.

You have to know what to write and how to say it, aware of the
fact that you sometimes just cannot put what you want to express
into words.

Risks.

It is time to say goodbye, and all I wish to do now is to thank
those who have made all this possible. The order in which I put
them will be casual and improvised:

My family for having put up with me on this journey;

Sabrina for having put up with me on this journey;

www.allenatore.net for the opportunity they have given me;

The directors of the Massa Lombarda youth section who had the
courage five years ago to entrust me with the technical guidance
of a soccer team;

A. C. Massa Lombarda, who gave me the chance to go on
coaching and to grow and develop as a coach and as a person;

All the coaches that I was lucky enough to be with during my experiences as a player (if that is not too important a word!);

All my former teammates;

All the young players that I have had the luck and the honor to train;

All those people, coaches or not, with whom I have spent hours and hours talking about soccer and not only that - drawing arrows and playing fields on napkins or pieces of paper or the windows of cars;

All those people who have influenced my life in one way or another;

Samuel, who has accompanied me on this 'psycho-kinetic' voyage;

And all those who have had or will have the interest, the curiosity or the chance to read this book.

Thanks.

Matteo Pernisa